CRIMINAL

ALEXIS ABBOTT

Get an EXCLUSIVE book, **FREE** just as a thank you for signing up for my newsletter! Plus you'll never miss a new release, cover reveal, or promotion!

http://alexisabbott.com/newsletter

"*Oh, Kaiden! Right there! Oh God, I'm going to come!*"

The rhythmic creak of the bed is the least of my worries as I lay awake, listening to them. My step-brother and... who's tonight's guest? I want to say Samantha, but honestly, they've all blurred together by this point.

The bed grinds into the floor, the headboard banging against the drywall. Kaiden's breathing is hard, but he doesn't say much at all. He just makes her scream louder.

All the women he takes back to his place might call out his name like he's some sex-God, but he barely ever makes a sound, let alone puts much effort into remembering their names. What's the point? I'd never seen the same girl by twice since I moved in with him six weeks ago.

Every night it's the same thing. I'd almost think it was a routine if Kaiden weren't so against such things.

He comes in around one or two in the morning with some new girl, usually tipsy, and both of them laughing before he takes them into his bedroom. And, unfortunately, his bed is right up against the paper-thin walls.

Right up against my room.

I pressed the pillow to my head as Samantha-or-whoever screams and Kaiden grunts.

"Take it," he growls. *"Take it all!"*

He doesn't care at all that I can hear. I'm under his roof and his control now, at least until I decide what to do with my life. Everything had been derailed when my father and step-mother—his bio-mom—died in a car accident eight months back. Before that, I thought everything was going to be fine. I had just turned eighteen, and I had an education fund set aside.

I didn't know that my education fund had been 'borrowed' from to bail Kaiden out of jail. I didn't realize that my parents were effectively broke. I also didn't realize how much funerals cost. And I had to do it all on my own. Kaiden barely even made an appearance outside of the funeral, and though he looked broken-hearted, he was gone before I could blink.

So instead of going off to college, all expenses

paid, I struggled to live on my own, grieving for months. Then the restaurant I worked at went bank-rupt. I had to beg my step-brother, the person who had bankrupted my college fund, for a place to stay.

And he was just as happy about it as I was. I was going to interfere with his life, he said.

What kind of life does he have, anyway? Screwing random women every night, making money in who-knows-what ways. He was arrested for drugs, but that bar he hangs out in every night, I knew that was trouble; that the people he hung out with were trouble.

What other choice do I have, though?

So I lay in bed, listening to him pound the girl into oblivion, and I can barely help the flush that goes through me. Beneath my annoyance and anger, there was hurt as well. Beneath it all, I can still remember how much I'd crushed on him through high school. How every time my friends told me how hot he was, I was secretly agreeing. I can still remember the time when we went boating, and I fell in. He rescued me, held my face, and all I wanted him to do was kiss me, but he didn't. He got all awkward and wouldn't talk to me for a week.

My body feels like it's floating as I hear them come, as if I weren't quite within myself, but looking down as I flush, my hand dips between my thighs.

It's not something I'm proud of. The way my body prickles with heat, craves my touch. It's a habit

I thought I'd broken. I had hoped it was just a childhood phase, but as I hear him grunt and growl, I can picture him laying over me, his gorgeous body thrusting.

The fantasy is so familiar, and I burn with desire.

I touch myself over my panties; my body is already so hot and wet, so needy from listening to my step-brother have sex with his latest fling. I close my eyes, holding in my moan so that he won't hear me. So that he won't know what I'm doing, fantasizing about him.

Every night I have to fight the urge to masturbate to the sounds of him pleasuring someone else. Every night I have to remind myself how dirty these desires are.

I swallow and force my hand away, so desperately wanting to lose myself in my fantasy.

But I can't.

* * *

MY SCHEDULE HAS BEEN TURNED UPSIDE-DOWN since I moved in with him. How can I get up bright and early to look for a job when he's been keeping me up 'til three in the morning screwing random chicks?

I plunk myself down at the kitchen table, a plate of toast and some tea in front of me.

Kaiden's still sleeping, even though it's past noon, and I at least have some peace and quiet. I bring the piece of toast to my lips as I boot up my laptop and the local job search pages.

I haven't been having any luck. Kaiden lives in the middle of nowhere, and just like Kaiden's nightly rituals, the job search page is always the same. Some jobs clearly out of my experience and education range, one or two scam postings, and that's it.

We don't even have a big chain store, not for an hour-long drive.

But today, there's something new.

The bar Kaiden is always at is looking for a shot-girl.

Let me be clear. I don't want to work at that dive. I don't want to be surrounded by the people he's surrounded by, and I certainly don't want to see my step-brother picking up chicks.

But I click it anyways, pushing aside my toast as I lean in.

Shot Girl Wanted!!!

Great tips, hourly wage $10. Must provide own uniform & be able to stand on feet for 10 hours. Call Ryder for more info.

I jot down the number just as Kaiden rises from his hibernation. He instantly snatches my laptop like he owns it, looking at the screen.

"Fuck off, Kaiden!" I spit out as I grab for it back. Not like it's going to do any good. Kaiden is six-foot-five and two-hundred-fifty pounds of muscle, easy.

I can't deny that I can see what other women see in him. The appeal of that kind of guy.

The one with muscles and pierced nipples, and who, for some horrible reason, decides to go around shirtless all the time around his house.

His house, his rules. That's his motto.

I just wish his body didn't drive me crazy.

"Hah, little Abigail a shot-girl? Yeah right," he says as he carelessly tosses the laptop back on the table, setting my tea to shaking. I reach out and grab it, glaring at him.

"Whatever, I could totally do it."

Besides, I need to if I'm ever going to earn enough money to find my own place. I need enough for a damage deposit and first and last rent, at least, and Kaiden has the nerve to charge me rent as well. Says I owe him, now.

As if he weren't the reason I was in this mess in the first place.

"Whatever, Princess," he says with a roll of his green eyes. He leans against the countertop, hands pressed into it and making his biceps bulge, his brown hair tousled and messy. Every time he speaks, I'm thrown by the little hint of his tongue piercing, which, as far as I know, he never uses on those girls.

And if anyone would know, it would be me. After all, I can hear everything in his room. It sets my stomach to turning.

Just as I'm about to bite something back at him

that would have been totally cutting, Samantha stumbles from his room, wearing nothing but his t-shirt that ends not even halfway past her ass.

"Damn it," I curse under my breath, grabbing my toast and stuffing the corner in my mouth as I take my laptop and tea into my hands.

By that time, Samantha's hand is already on his chest, possessively, and she's glaring at me with her dark eyes. Her red hair is wild and frizzy, her nose ring glinting in the mid-day sun.

"Who's she?" she spits out, sizing me up.

I'm everything she isn't. My eyes are bright blue, and my blonde hair is stick-straight and neatly clipped back. Plus, I'm wearing a dressy blouse and a skirt. I'm not joking around about needing a job, and I believe in dressing the part.

"My sister," Kaiden says, his lips permanently crooked in a smirk.

"Step-sister," I retort quickly. I don't want anyone to think we'd come from the same stock.

"Oh. Hi." Samantha looks at Kaiden as if expecting he'd say more. Maybe make her some coffee.

But his eyes are on me, that smirk of his is never fading as his newest fling felt him up, and I wonder if he gets off on torturing me. Knowing I can hear him and that I can't sleep because of his sexual antics.

"Whatever, you don't have to be nice to me.

Kaiden'll never have you back."

Her eyes narrow at me.

"What the fuck did you say to me?"

I roll my eyes. I'm just as bad as Kaiden with that. Maybe growing up together did rub off on me a little, though I hate to admit we're anything alike.

"I said he's a pump-it and dump-it kinda guy. But since you were faking it last night, that won't be a problem, right?"

I'm pushing it, and I know it. I give Kaiden a glance before I shut my bedroom door, but I swear, he looks impressed.

And then all I can hear is Samantha screaming at him about how he used her.

I'll have to wait to call Ryder about the shot-girl position, but knowing the crowd he runs with, he probably isn't up yet anyway.

"We'll need to see you in person."

I nod, even though I'm on the phone. It's so embarrassing to do that, but I'm gratefully alone. After Kaiden had given Samantha his standard, 'It was nice but that's all it was,' speech, he'd taken off as well, and I'm finally alone to savor the quiet. At least there's that in this small town. Quiet.

When my step-brother isn't fucking any random woman he meets inches from my head.

"Of course!" I tell Ryder, hoping that my smile is audible. "When should I come over?"

"Tonight, seven o'clock. Come dressed to work; if we like you, you start tonight."

"Absolutely, I'll be there. Thank you so much, Ryder."

He doesn't reply, and then there's nothing but the emptiness of a hang-up. My stomach is in knots. I look at my phone. It's already three in the afternoon, and I don't have any clothes that scream *shot-girl*. Everything I have is, well, proper. Prim. And at the bar that Kaiden frequents? Prim isn't going to cut it.

That, in and of itself, is bad enough. But I just have to get over my prudishness for a little while. A couple of months of work, and I should have enough saved up to get out of this place and be somewhere more comfortable. I'll find a nice roommate in a big city, a better job...

It's all a stepping stone.

I grab my keys and head for the door. I have to get to a mall.

* * *

I'M STRAPPED FOR CASH. That is the nice way of saying it.

At my last job, I'd managed to save a whopping $127.83. I'd begged Kaiden to let me off with rent until I found a new job, but he's getting impatient.

After gas and expenses, I have only $89.26 to my name, and I have to make it count. I need this job like I'd never needed anything else, and all my moral quarrels are going to have to be pushed to the side for the moment. I walk into the trashy little strip mall, into a used clothing store. That disgusts me too. It isn't that I'm prissy, I swear, even if Kaiden won't stop calling me Princess. But my dad had always been closer to the upper side of middle class.

We had a nice house and a nice car, and more debt than I could've ever figured. The bank fore-closed on the house even as I desperately tried to pay the inflated mortgage, but I managed to keep the car.

At least there's that because it gets good mileage and is big enough that I was able to sleep in it those few days when things got really dark.

I flick through the racks, looking for something that will make me stand out. I know that looking like a suburban cheerleader isn't going to work in my favor unless I look a little, well, maybe "trashy" is an ugly word, but...

My hands fall on a scarlet tank top that looks like it'll barely cover my chest, and I pause. It's only $4.

I toss it in the cart, along with a couple other choices, followed by more miniskirts than I've ever owned, before moving towards the shoes.

If I'm going to be standing, I know I'd have to dress practically, but the white sneakers that draw my eyes just aren't going to cut it.

Since I went to a school that had a uniform, I don't have a lot of options for sexy shoes.

I roam along the shoe aisle, but there's nothing. Worn flip-flops, brown shoes that look too out-of-fashion for even a senior to wear, and some scuffed-up pumps that look like their heels are hanging on by threads.

Old shoes skeeve me out at the best of times, but seeing the sad selection before me is a miserable disappointment. Shoes are already so expensive, and I don't want to spend all of my meagre budget on it.

But what options do I have? I need them.

I sigh and make my way towards the changing rooms, quickly trying on the clothes. Over half are discarded as being either too baggy or not sexy enough. But the scarlet tank top and a couple of the miniskirts are perfect, and I feel a bit better about it all. At least this way I save some money on the clothes.

I'm about to head to the checkout when something catches my eye. I move over towards the furniture section, and for a moment, all I can do is stare.

There is the exact dresser I had as a kid. I can't believe it. I mean, I'm sure it isn't the exact one, but it looks just like it. My fingers run along the top of the white painted wood, feeling it with a sense of melancholic joy.

Along with the house, all of my possessions went with it—anything I couldn't take with me in the car.

I couldn't even afford storage, and my dad and step-mom never really had any family they were close to.

I miss mom and dad. There's no denying that. I've just been struggling to stay afloat, and every reminder of them gives me a sharp pain in my chest. All I want to do is curl up in my bed, but ever since they passed, it's just been disaster after disaster. I haven't even had a moment to mourn them, and Kaiden... I guess he's doing the guy thing. Pretending it doesn't affect him.

But I can see it in his eyes, that shadow. He misses them too.

I smile a little, just at the familiarity of an object that reminds me of happier times. Of when they were still alive, and we were still a family.

I idly open the top drawer to find that there must have been someone who had stowed away some finds that they couldn't afford. A bundle of clothes.

I'm just about to close it when something shiny draws my gaze. Black patent leather.

I push the clothes aside and hidden beneath is a pair of stiletto platforms like I've never seen. They're gorgeous, not a smudge or scratch on them. But I know better than to hope they're my size.

When I lift them and look at the bottom, not only are they my size, but they're only $6! I'm about to jump for joy, but instead I shove them in my basket, beaming all the way to the checkout line.

Maybe this is meant to be after all.

I'm so nervous. I look up at the seedy bar, and my heart is racing. It looks so grungy. The sign is crooked, and the light above the door keeps flickering in and out.

If I was watching a horror movie, this is the time that I'd be screaming at the character to get out of there while she could.

But I haven't gotten another interview in six weeks, Kaiden wants me to pay up or get out, and I have no where else to go.

I push up my bra, tugging down the front of the tank top a little and pray for my pushup to do a little bit better of a job tonight. I'm a solid A-cup usually, which is an annoyance on a normal day, but if it costs me a job, that'll be a whole other thing.

I haven't seen Kaiden since I got home, which I'm grateful for. The last thing I want to deal with is his questions and smartass comments about how I'm not cut out to be a shot girl. I've heard enough of that since I got the call for the interview.

He doesn't believe I'm cut out for it. I'm too *perfect,* in his words, though he says it like the word is poison on his tongue.

Little miss perfect.

He just hates that I always got straight A's in school. A lot of good that does me now, considering everything that has happened.

My interview is in five minutes. I'd gotten here twenty minutes early, and now I'm just waiting for the right time.

I am bright enough to know that showing up early isn't likely to earn me any brownie points in this place. If the owner is anything like Kaiden, you don't waste someone's time by showing up late... or early.

But I watch as the time on my car dashboard slowly clicks down the minutes of my life as my anxiety grows. Maybe I can't do it. Maybe I'm not good enough.

Maybe I am just too *perfect* and should just try to apply for some scholarships and go back to school, in a strange place, where I know no one, and no one knows me. Hell, if I leave the state, Kaiden couldn't even follow me if he wanted, thanks to the conditions of his bail.

There's a strange sense of enjoyment I take in the

thoughts of starting anew, but a part of me doesn't want to. For all the stuff Kaiden puts me through, he is still the only family I have left.

And I don't want to lose him again. Even if being near him drives me crazy.

The clock turns six fifty-nine, and I leave the vehicle.

Tugging down my skirt and tank top, I look at myself once more in the rear-view mirror. I can hardly recognize myself, with my dark shadowed eyes, heavy mascara, and red lipstick. I teased up my hair a bit too, or at least tried to, to give it more volume, and I hope it doesn't look as bad to Ryder as it looks to me.

I take a deep breath.

Here goes everything.

Walking towards the door, I look at the flickering light, and the sense of foreboding churns in my stomach, but I push it aside.

But just then, two people push their way out of the bar, making out and completely ignorant to my presence. Her hands are all over him, and she is *grinding* on him. Right there in the parking lot as he slams her up against the wall.

She giggles, and he growls, and as I get closer, I think I'm going to be sick.

"Kaiden?" I practically shout, and I want to run closer, but the heels are way higher than anything

I've walked in before, and I have to take each step gingerly, especially on the uneven asphalt.

He doesn't stop as he sucks face with the latest floozy. I already know it isn't the one from last night, or the night before, or the night before that.

He pins her hands above her head before he finally turns to look at me, shooting me the most arrogant, cocky look I've ever seen on his face.

Did he time this just to piss me off?

I scowl at him as I push past them, yanking on the door with a "Whatever" thrown in their direction.

It would've been really smooth and badass if the door didn't choose that moment to get stuck. I yank on it and, of course, it sends me backward, my heels giving way beneath me as I drop unceremoniously to the greasy asphalt.

I'm ready to sink into the ground when I hear her laughter. My cheeks burn hot until suddenly I can feel Kaiden's rough hands on my bare shoulders, hoisting me up as he tosses a "Shut up" at his most recent fling.

She obeys, but I'm already humiliated, and tears sting my eyes.

"I told you — you aren't cut out for this," he whispers in my ear, his words dark and low so that she couldn't hear him.

I want to punch him. The nerve!

Instead, I tug on the door again, and it blissfully opens as I pull myself away from him.

"I didn't ask for your opinion," I remind him as I step inside.

I have to blink as my eyes adjust to the dim light, but the bigger adjustment is the smell of stale beer and vomit.

This is not a place for someone like me. I know that. Honestly, if Kaiden weren't standing right outside the door believing that I couldn't do it, I'd turn around right now. I'm terrified, and it's gross in here.

I look at the few rickety chairs and booths, the fabric torn and some of the chairs looking as if they'd been broken and haphazardly put back together. It's a place where more than a few bar fights happened.

A place an eighteen-year-old has no business being.

I push myself forward, trying to look confident as I teeter in my heels over to the bar. The floor is sticky and makes a sickly sound that I can feel as well as hear over the noise of loud rock music playing out of a jukebox past its prime.

There are a few guys at the bar, hard and mean looking with grizzled faces and beer bellies, but their expressions soften as they look me over in the lewdest way.

I guess "soften" isn't the right word.

I look behind the bar at the greasy-looking man with the thin mustache and the long, black hair and give him what I hope to be a glowing smile. I don't want to look apprehensive or terrified, or to give away any of my impressions of him, about his patrons, or about his job.

"Hi! I'm looking for Ryder?"

I guess Ryder was looking out for me, or maybe just has cameras in his little dive, because the words are barely out of my mouth when I feel a tap on my shoulder. I turn to see a towering, blond man.

"You're looking for me, hun," he says, his words patronizing, but his deep voice making it seem natural. Just like how Kaiden speaks to women.

He's broad and built more like a bodyguard than an owner, but I guess they sometimes double up.

I stare up at him, and I can't help but be a little shocked. He's not like the slimy patrons or the greasy bartender. He is probably thirty-five if I was to guess, and if it weren't for the scar that nipped the top of his lip, he'd be flawless. Like, model-flawless.

"Oh! Right, yes, hi," I say with a bright smile, offering him my hand. "I'm Abigail; we talked on the phone?"

"Yeah, I remember. Shot-girl," he says as his steely eyes wander up and down my body, inspecting me like I'm a piece of meat. It made my stomach turn when the others did it, but when he does, it's something different.

I like it a little bit. It's flattering.

I don't want to think about what that says about me, and I don't get a chance to. Kaiden pushes his way into the bar, without the brunette he'd been so recently sucking face with.

He looks at me with his green eyes, his tall and broad body so imposing in the small space. But I shift my gaze back to Ryder, forcing a confident grin on my made-up lips.

I'm an imposter. I'm not a twenty-one-year-old girl, and I don't go around in dark eyeshadow, low-cut tops, short skirts and towering heels.

But I'm going to act like I am.

"You said I could start tonight?"

"Yeah," Ryder says in that deep voice of his. "Yeah, you can start tonight."

He doesn't ask for my ID, my references, nothing. Just like that.

I feel so relieved, almost smug, until I look at Kaiden's face and see the anger brewing beneath the surface.

I guess he's going to have to find another place to pick up chicks if his little sister is going to be around all the time.

That gives me a little bit of joy too.

* * *

MY LEGS ARE KILLING ME. All night was spent standing, walking around from one table of middle-aged men to another, the bar littered with younger men who're trying to suck up to Ryder, from the looks of things.

And to my surprise, the place is packed with women.

Women who call me sugar-tits and spank my ass as I walked by, just like the men. As if they're one in the same.

Women who wear too much perfume and chew gum with their mouth open, and men who leer at everything and smoke pot wherever they please.

It's like working in the Wild West. No law, no order, no nothing.

I'd have been out of there a dozen times over if it wasn't for the fact that my tip purse is risking over-flowing.

I haven't seen Ryder or Kaiden in a while, but time is passing so fast.

The town is small, but I swear, most of the people in it are in the bar tonight. I've lived in this place for six weeks and barely see anyone except for at the stores, and I guess I know why now. They're spending all their time here.

And they're all spending their hard-earned money on drinks and tips, and if I'm not being bliss-fully unaware, I'd guess a little something extra. But I have to turn my head on that because I don't want to get involved in any dirty business.

But when Kaiden emerges from the back office, his face red as he makes his way over to me, I feel a bit scared. My brother is towering, to say the least, and he looks pissed.

His hand wraps around my upper arm as he stares down on me, and I can tell he's already drawing the eyes of the crowd. There's a tense energy in the air, like everyone's waiting for something like this to happen.

He bends down, leaning in towards my ear and practically growling at me.

"You gotta come home with me. Now," he says, his strong hand tightening around my bicep. His hand is huge, just like the rest of him, and it encircles my thin arm easily.

Still, I try to yank it away.

"Buzz off, Kaiden," I hiss back. "I'm doing this for *you*, remember?" I spit though it's only half true. Sure, I need money to pay him for rent, but I also need money for my own stuff, like moving out and getting a real place to stay in a real city.

He won't let me go, though, and starts dragging me to the door. I'm helpless against his strength, and even as I try to yank my arm back, nearly stumbling to my ass, he just keeps dragging me like I'm a dog on his leash.

I am humiliated beyond compare, even though most of the crowd is probably too drunk and high to remember much of tonight.

Still, it's the principle of the thing.

When the cold air of the outside hits my lungs, and the flashing light above the door spins eerie shadows around us, he finally lets me go as if I wouldn't just run back inside.

I guess he's right on that count because I don't. I don't want my older brother dragging me out of the bar again.

"What the hell, Kaiden?" I spit out as he takes a few steps away from me, putting distance between us. I don't know if it's because he's afraid of me or, more likely, afraid of what he's going to do if I'm too close. The thought sends a shiver down my spine.

"You can't work here," he says.

And I roll my eyes with exasperation.

"You aren't the boss of me," I say, and anger starts welling up within my chest. Is that what this is all about? "And I got this dumb job to pay your rent since apparently letting your sister live with you when she's *homeless* is such an inconvenience to you!"

"It *is* a fucking inconvenience." He spins about and glares at me, his green eyes flashing with anger. "And you have no idea what you're talking about. What it's like in there," he says, pointing his finger at the closed door as his other hand runs through his hair.

I wonder if he's been drinking. He'd disappeared a long time, after all.

"I know what it's like, Kaiden. I'm not a baby, and I'm just doing it for the money, not because I want to be like *you*."

I feel bad throwing that in his face, but it's true. I don't want the lifestyle he has. I don't want to come to a bar just to hang out, to waste my life away and chill out with my friends.

Not that I have any friends.

He sneers at me, and it gives him such a perfect "bad boy" look it's uncanny. Like out of a movie.

That makes me hate him more because I know exactly why all the girls want him. Despite his assholish arrogance, he has the body and the face that lets him get away with murder.

Well, not quite, considering his bail. But close enough.

"If this is just about rent, you walk in there right now and tell Ryder you're through. You can't cut it," he orders. And if I were anyone else, I likely would've backed down.

But I am his sister, and he owes me. More than owes me.

I reach into my purse, taking out the wads of dollar bills, flashing them to his face.

"Look! Rent! Aren't you happy now, Kaiden? I'm not a liability anymore," I sneer right back, and by now I'm pissed.

He is the reason I couldn't go to college; he is the

reason I had to take this job, and now he's trying to force me to quit?

He can't control every aspect of my life, damn it!

He's breathing heavily, and he takes a few steps closer to me. He has over a foot on me usually, but in my heels, I come up almost to his shoulders though he's over one hundred pounds of muscle more than me too.

Kaiden is an intimidating guy.

But he'd never hurt me. Not like that.

"Abigail, I mean it," he says darkly.

I take a step backward and shake my head.

"You can't tell me what to do, Kaiden. Get over it," I say as I shove the money back in my purse.

He reaches out, grabbing my face and forcing me to look at him, and there is so much emotion in his expression that I don't understand. Couldn't comprehend. The intensity behind his eyes is unlike anything I'd ever seen, and it gives me pause.

But then he releases me and storms back into the club, leaving me alone in the chilly, dark outside to catch my breath.

It's been a hard week, and not just because I've worked every day. That would be hard in and of itself, especially in the heels that were killing my feet.

It was hard because dealing with drunks brings about a sort of mental exhaustion I haven't felt before. Seeing their faces day after day and catching that haunted unhappiness between the hoots and the hollers, it takes a toll.

But I think the worst part of it is that Kaiden is avoiding me. He sneaks in after I've gone to bed. There hasn't been any women. No sex. Nothing to incite my rage.

And he hasn't talked to me since our fight at the club. It's driving me crazy, and I didn't think that it could affect me like it is. I'm torn up about it. The worst part is I barely even know why. I guess it's because I'm invading 'his' place, but even that doesn't wholly make sense. There's something else going on between us, and I have no idea what.

I give another drunk a gin, and he grabs my ass before handing me a ten-dollar bill with a leering grin. I feel like I'm going to be sick to my stomach, and when I try to tug the bill out of his hand, he tightens his grasp.

"I'll do it for a kiss," he says, puckering up his weathered lips and looking at me through his watery eyes with expectation.

But I'm not that desperate, and I let it go, turning my back on him. I need some air, and I look at the bartender, motioning that I'm heading out for a second.

Opening the door, I find the eerie light to be strangely soothing, but when I hear a motorcycle's engine rev up, I quickly move away from the entrance and the parking lot towards the back.

I can hear some voices though I can't make them out yet.

Maybe I'm stupid, but I'm getting curious, and I try to make soft steps as I move towards them. I hold my breath, and it's like by instinct I know I shouldn't be here. As if I'm tiptoeing up to my parent's bedroom at night, trying to hear what they're saying about us.

"Man, I'm already looking at three years,

minimum, for you." I recognized the voice just as clear as day.

Kaiden.

I press myself up against the wall of the building, breathing softly through my nose. I can't hear who replies or what they say as the motorcycle gets nearer. He seems to be parked in the lot, revving the engine for some reason.

My ears strain, and I hear Kaiden's voice again.

"You know what this means," he says, his tone threatening and dark.

But then there's another deep voice I recognize, and it's like my blood turns cold in my veins.

"You want to play that game with me, boy? Fine. But just remember that your little sister is here, and if you screw me, well... I'll screw her. In more than one way."

Ryder.

I bite down on my lower lip so hard that it feels like it's going to start bleeding at any second, and tears are threatening my eyes.

It's stupid to be so sensitive over something like this, but I can't help it. I've always been the sensitive one, not strong like Kaiden or my dad.

There's a long pause, and I can picture Kaiden, his face contorted in... what? Would he be angry at that?

I don't honestly know. Maybe he thinks it's funny, just a joke.

But when I hear his voice, it removes all doubt from my mind.

"If you touch a hair on her head, you're going to wish you killed me when you had the chance, you smug fucking prick," he growls, his voice low and hard. I've never heard him sound quite like it, but more than that... he almost got killed?

My stomach turns to lead as I take a step backward. Do I want to hear more? *Can* I hear more?

My mind is fuzzy as I try to remain calm, to not let emotions overtake me.

"Yeah, well, there's still time you punk. You fuck up on the stand, it's not your life you're going to have to be worried about. Think of Abigail as... collateral."

"You're not going to touch her," Kaiden threatens, and I take another step towards the parking lot. "You touch her, and I will fucking dismember you, to hell with Axel's orders."

Who's Axel? I shake my head. I can't take any more. I turn and head back into the bar and the stale stench of beer and alcohol and leering faces.

But for the rest of the night, I'm completely unable to concentrate. Especially when I see Ryder come in a bit later, asking for ice and holding it to his swollen jaw.

For a second, I think that maybe I should've stayed longer and heard what it was that finally set Kaiden off, but I knew that I'd be better off not knowing. Though left to wonder about it and worry is an even worse fate, sometimes.

I don't see Kaiden the rest of the night, but when I get home, his bike is in the driveway, and I pull up behind it.

Am I going to say anything about what I heard? That I understand now why he didn't want me to work there? Hell, is this why he didn't want me to come at all?

Maybe Kaiden had kept my identity a secret to protect me, and that was why he was fighting so hard to keep me away from him.

And then I wonder something worse... was this why Ryder was looking for a shot-girl in the first place? Did he lure me in close, just to have this over Kaiden's head?

My mind races with the possibilities, the strange layers that never occurred to me even to think about before. Is this why Kaiden had been so adamant about me not working at the bar?

Was that all to protect me?

"Look, one more fuckup like that and Ryder's gonna can your ass," Kaiden says with a sneer. His lips curve upward as he stares down at me like I'd just vomited on his shoes.

He is pissed, and all I did was tell a guy not to

spank my ass. I'm getting tired of being treated like meat around this place, but honestly, I'm terrified of leaving.

Not just of what me leaving would do to myself, but my brother as well. Step-brother.

I have to keep reminding myself of that now, because ever since I heard him out back with Ryder, I've started softening towards him. Even though this is the third time this week I've had to hear him tell me off.

"It's nothing," I say with a roll of my eyes. I'm trying to act natural as if I hadn't heard what was said that night. It was almost a week ago, now. I never got a chance to talk to him about it because he's in his room by the time I get home, and then gone before I get up the next morning.

I have no idea what he's been doing, but his erratic behavior is scaring me now.

I lick my lips, tucking some of my blonde hair behind my ear and trying to stand up tall and straight. Look strong. Intimidating.

"It's not okay, Abigail. You're on thin ice as it is."

People are looking at us, but by this point, I think they've come to expect fights between us. Every day for the past week he's been doing something to shame me in front of the customers. Every minor indiscretion was worthy of his telling me off in public, despite him not being my boss.

I get why he's doing it, but that doesn't mean I'm not sick of it.

"Listen, *Kaiden*, that's sexual harassment in the workplace, and if I'm supposed to put up with that, then I need to be making a lot more than $10 an hour. I'm not a stripper, and if I were? I'd probably be making a lot more!"

He blanches, and I'm proud of myself for a second. I like it when I can get in under his skin in revenge for all the times he's done it to me.

He reaches out, grabbing my upper arm and staring down at me.

"Listen, Abigail, just get the fuck outta here. Go back to school, do whatever goody-goody shit you wanna do, but you can't cut it in this place. If you don't want gross old guys grabbin' your ass, this isn't the job for you, *Princess*. Just like I told you a million times before."

I tug my arm, but he holds tight and my lip twitches. He's so strong, and he's always doing little things to remind me of that and intimidate me.

"I can do this, Kaiden. I've been doing it for two weeks now, without a break. I'm tired, my legs hurt, and your attitude isn't helping right now."

"Doesn't sound to me like you can cut it, *Princess*."

His green eyes flash at me, along with that pierced tongue of his, and he thinks he has me in the corner. That I'm going to back down at any second, but I refuse. I'm not going to do that.

I can't!

I mean, part of it is my pride, but not for a moment do I think that if I disappeared, Ryder would forget about me. Or that he'd forget about Kaiden's potential to screw him over.

Oh my God, if I left, Ryder might even think that Kaiden had hidden me away just so that he could tell the judge or whoever about Ryder's business! About the attempted murder or threat or whatever it was that spooked Kaiden so bad.

I'm trembling as I stare up at him, but I lean in close, my body pressing against his as I angle my lips to his ear.

"You're not getting rid of me so easy, Kaiden," I swear, and I lower myself back to the floor, daring him to disagree.

He finally releases me before picking up the nearest pint glass and tossing it at the wall.

I shake and squeak as it shatters, flying into dozens of pieces.

Before I can even gather my words, though, he's storming out the front door and leaving me to clean up his mess.

I've seen him mad before. Violent, even. But this is way more intense than anything else.

I move towards the nearest shards, starting to sweep them up with the grimy broom and dustpan as the rest of the bar goes back to their conversations. The music is loud and has a little bit of static to it, and it's getting on my nerves, just like everything else here.

Just like everyone else here.

I don't realize how fast I was breathing until I lean against the wall with the glass in the dustpan and feel my heart racing.

I know Kaiden's only trying to protect me, but I'm trying to protect him, too. We're all each other has...

ABIGAIL

The day I hate working most, so far, is always Saturday. I don't know what it is. The run-of-the-mill Monday-Thursday drunks I'm getting used to, but Friday and Saturday night? It's as if everyone is on cocaine.

Which, I guess, is entirely plausible.

I move to the next table, tray of drinks perched on my arm as I smile. A woman who's here every night smiles at me with her orange lips and blue eyes, taking her gin and tonic.

"Thanks, honey," she says with an exaggerated wink. She's always hoping I'll let her know who the big spenders are, and she's always nice, so sometimes I point her in the direction of someone especially hammered.

Despite how much I hate being called honey,

she's one of the better customers, and I smile at her, then at the two other women at her side.

"Shots, ladies?" I ask with a phony grin. It's only eleven, and I have four more hours of this routine before I can finally, blissfully relax. And despite it breaking, like, every state law I know of, Ryder's acting like giving me Sunday off is a favor, after working seventeen shifts in a row.

I can't wait just to soak in a tub and not have to go into work. I was thin when I started, but now I have muscles in places I never did before, my calves and arms more sculpted.

But no one can say I don't suffer for my figure.

"Yes! We're *celebrating!*" the blonde to my regular's left says with a smile as she reaches up with grabby hands towards the tray.

"Everything you have!" the blonde says way too loud, but I smile politely and quickly count up the drinks on my tray.

"It's $65 for the lot," I say with a smile, and the blonde throws me a crisp, $100 bill.

"Keep the change!"

And if there's any way to a waitress' heart, it's that.

I smile as I put the tray down on the table before tucking the $35 into my pocket. I bring the rest to the register and go back to grab more shots.

Maybe tonight isn't going to be so bad.

Though when I hear the hooping and hollering in

the back, I get a prickle down my spine, and I immediately know how wrong I am.

I'm used to drunk guys, high guys, loud guys, and leering guys, but once you're around them enough, you know the signs. The slight, little differences between someone just being drunk, and someone being *dangerously* drunk.

Between someone being high, and someone being stoned out of their mind.

Between a guy being loud and perverted... and *those* guys.

I glance over my shoulder at them, feeling the dread begin to build in the pit of my stomach as I top off the last of my shots.

They're at the table with the regular and her friends, skimming drinks from them. That, on its own? Normal night.

But the way he's touching blondie sends a chill up my spine.

Ryder's behind the bar, just watching placidly, as if simply waiting to see what I'd do. And knowing what I know about him... I don't want to do a single thing to upset him or earn his ire.

So when he turns his head to look at me, his brow raised, I know it's time for action.

I take the steps across the bar, returning to where I was just moments before, and I give the loudest, leeringest, drunkest guy I've ever seen my most dazzling smile. He's clearly over twice my age and looks older than that, with the heavy lines and the vacant, blue eyes.

He's a guy that's seen a lot of hatred and hard times, that's for sure.

"Did you need more drinks?" I ask politely, begging my voice not to quiver, but my intuition is telling me he's not a good man. He's not someone I should even be talking to or getting the attention of.

"Well hi there, *precious*," he says with a slur and a wobble as he removes his hand from blondie's shoulder to go for mine. He's off balance and nearly falls over, supported only by me. He makes me nearly spill all my shots as he does, and I cry out.

I just made a $35 tip, and I didn't want it all to go to replacing spilled drinks by this asshole.

He doesn't seem to notice or care, though, and I quickly put down the tray on an empty table as he fumbles.

And just as I rise back up, he grabs my breast. Not accidentally.

My face is red with rage as he squeezes it in his hand, letting out the most disgusting moan I've ever heard in my life.

"What a ripe peach," he shudders as I try to back up, but I'm pinned between him and the bench, and the ladies to my left are just laughing like it's all a joke.

I grab onto the bench, trying to push myself up, but he's built strong, and I can't move as he puts more weight on me. His entire body is pinning me down, holding me there as he squeezes my breast so hard it hurts like he's bruising me.

I let out a shout, and just as he's about to bring his other hand up, headed towards my thigh, there's a scuffling of tables. I can't see anything beyond the disgusting drunk until he's yanked off me and thrown to the ground. Hard.

The thud can be heard even over the music, over the laughter of the drunk women next to me, over my screams.

And then Kaiden is atop him, pummeling his face over and over, and even though I've never been in a real fistfight, I can tell he's not holding back.

Each time they connect, they make a sick cracking noise, and I cringe away. I feel like I'm going to be sick, and I finally manage to jump up— around the two of them and between the tables, out the door into the night air. My hands go to my knees, and I buckle over, dry heaving onto the asphalt.

Tears sting my eyes, embarrassment and anger combining in me.

I don't know how long I stay, just trying not to throw up, but suddenly there's a hand on my back, and I jump, startled, away from him.

"It's just me, Abby," says a much softer, tenderer voice than I'm used to. I haven't heard Kaiden sound like that in so long...

"Listen, we gotta go," he says, taking a step nearer to me, but I back away.

"I'm fine, Kaiden. I didn't need your help," I spit back, and my words sting him like acid. He visibly flinches, and some part of me feels bad, but I'm too angry and scared to care.

"That fuck-head is still in there. He's a friend of Ryder's, you're not safe here," he warns, and his voice is starting to return to its normal hard, gravelly sound.

"I'm not leaving, I still have a shift to finish," I repeat, obstinate, and I can see the anger building in him too.

I glance down and notice the blood on his knuckles, and I know that by tomorrow, he'd be bruised and bandaged.

"I'm not fucking letting you go back in there tonight, Abby, so stop fighting me," he grunts, grabbing my shoulder roughly. And I just let him, even though the last thing I want is to be touched right now. But in a strange way, it's comforting.

Familiar.

Warm.

It's something I want, and something I don't want to want, all at once.

"I need the money," I protest weakly with a sob, but it's about more than that.

It's about what I heard him say to Ryder, what Ryder said back. It's about the fact that I'm already involved in something far more dangerous than some disgusting drunk.

"I remember when you looked up to me," Kaiden barks angrily, glaring daggers at me as he shakes my shoulder. "You remember that, huh? Remember, you used to call me your hero and mean it?"

Oh, I remember.

I was just a kid the first time I was picked on. I can't remember why anymore, but I remember being so upset I cried for days until Kaiden finally got it out of me.

The next time the kid started pushing me around, Kaiden was there. He got suspended for a week; his face was all bruised and he was so sore, but he just kept telling me he'd do it again for me. That he'd protect me.

No matter what.

Tears sting my eyes as I remember, and I try to brush past him, but he holds me still, his other hand going to my chin and forcing my watery eyes to look at him.

"What happened to that girl, Abby? The one who looked up to me?" He looks so sad, and his brows are furrowed as he holds my chin between his thumb and his index finger.

My eyes move from his, down to his lips. They're so near to me, so preciously near, and I envision myself just leaning forward. Pressing my mouth to his, thanking him for protecting me, for rescuing me.

Begging him to take me home and shield me from all the terrible things in the world.

I lick my lips, my breathing hard, and I'm not sure of how much time has passed, but it feels like an eternity before I finally pull away, bringing my gaze back to the ground.

"Things have changed, Kaiden," I say, icily. I can't have these feelings, and so I push him away, even though it breaks my heart. I can't look at his lips and think about kissing him.

It's wrong.

But even as I turn my back on him, my heart's racing, and a small part of me hopes he won't let me go.

* * *

I GET off my shift late, and luckily, the drunk was too wounded to hassle me anymore. And the ladies gave me an extra $50 to apologize for his behavior, though honestly, I just wanted them not to laugh at me while I was being assaulted.

I took a shower immediately after getting home, and now I feel like I'm suffocating from the overly hot water, wrapped in just a towel.

I'm crumpled up on my bed, and shocker, Kaiden isn't home yet. It's nice, in some ways, having the place to myself, though tonight I wanted him to be home, despite how I treated him. I was just so angry and embarrassed and... scared. Scared of what he was into with Ryder. Scared of what *I'm* into with Ryder.

I close my eyes, trying to find sleep, but instead, all I can find is the memory of his lips, hovering so near to me. A little split down the center from some fight or another, but still so full and gorgeous.

I moan softly as I think of his words, of how he and I used to be best friends. How he always took care of me before he just cut me out. It wasn't for a bad reason, I guess. He fell in with the wrong crowd and wants to protect me from their retribution. And the thought that he's so worried for me, so thoughtful, makes me smile even if it is messed up.

I smell like his body wash, and I have to admit... it's enticing in ways it shouldn't be.

I've dealt with these feelings for so long, but living with him, just the two of us alone, has brought them back to the surface. It's getting harder and harder to deny them. I don't even realize that my legs have parted, and that my hand is slowly snaking down the fluffy, white towel.

Maybe I should feel traumatized about what happened at the bar, and I do. I don't ever want to have to go back to work again. But I'm almost in shock, and all I can think about is Kaiden and how he'd rescued me, and how much I'd just wanted to kiss him. To let myself go and get wrapped up in him.

But that would require him to feel the same way, and he doesn't.

My fingers brush against my sex, and I let out a soft gasp of surprised pleasure. I'm already wet.

I imagine him coming into the room, finding me as I am, and walking over. His chest bare, his tattoos on display, as he licks his lips, running the piercing over it seductively.

He doesn't say anything. He doesn't have to. The expression on his face says it all as he looks over my freshly showered body, just the towel hiding me from his hungry, green eyes.

His hands touch on both of my knees as he leans on the bed, making it slant towards him as he puts his weight between me.

And then he leans down between my legs, kissing my clean little pussy, rubbing that tongue stud over my clit. I moan, my nipples stiffening beneath the towel as he reaches up beneath the fabric.

His hand dances along my stomach, loosening the towel as he reaches up and up before finding my small breast.

He's gentle, kind, exploring it with a tenderness I wouldn't expect from such a massive man. He lets out a growl between my legs as he begins lashing against my clit with more urgency. He looks up at me from between my legs, and I swear, they glitter with such passion and desire as if he's been waiting just as long for this as I have.

Thoughts of those broad, muscular shoulders rippling as he grasps my legs so tight and works his mouth over my pussy fill my mind. His big, powerful body focused upon me and mine, every rippling cord of sinew bulging as he lashes at my pussy.

An orgasm rushes through me unlike I've felt in a very long time. I don't know if he could've got me off so fast if he were actually eating me out.

"Oh, **Kaiden!**" I cry out, my body arching and aching as I tremble atop my bed, bucking my hips into my hand as the fantasy disappears. I'm left alone in my small room, just the feeling of shame burning through my body.

I blush as I come down, inwardly reprimanding myself.

You swore you wouldn't fantasize about him anymore.

I sneer at the unwanted thought.

The last thing I need right now is my brain telling me off for feeling good for the first time in months. And it's only a fantasy, something that will never happen. Something I'll never let happen.

I get up, dropping my towel and changing into my nightgown, but just as I'm about to crawl back into bed, I hear a motorcycle coming down the road.

You should apologize, I told myself, even though with my skin still flushed from the orgasm that I fantasized he gave me. I knew it was the right thing.

I didn't treat him fairly, and if I'm going to be staying much longer, I'm going to need to make it right. To thank him for standing up for me and protecting me, to let him know that I appreciate his concern. That things are good between us.

But when he comes in with the blonde woman that had tipped me earlier, the same one who laughed at me as I was being assaulted?

All bets are off.

"What the *fuck* Kaiden?!" I screech, looking from him to her, feeling absolutely and utterly humiliated once more. Here I am getting off to the thought of him, thinking of how caring and sweet he was, and he just has to come home with another floozy? The same floozy that embarrassed me not six hours earlier?

"Oh, Abigail. I didn't realize you'd still be up," he says, his voice reeking of disappointment as he goes to the fridge and grabs himself a beer. "You want something?" he asks the woman he was with.

She half stumbles around before leaning against the kitchen table and stares at Kaiden's ass. "I'm good, sugar," she coos, her voice slurred, and I want to smack her.

"I want her out of our house right now," I scream, more pissed that Kaiden seems so calm.

He stands upright, pulling off the cap of the beer bottle with his bare hands, taking a long drink.

It looks like he's already had a few from the way his face is flushed, and that pisses me off even more.

He looks between me and his 'date' for the night, shrugging his shoulders.

"Get out," he orders her, casually.

"What?" She looks confused, not sure if it's a joke, and she laughs. "You know I don't have a ride."

"Call your old man, then," he says, tossing her his cell phone. "He can pick you up on the way."

Maybe it's the way he's looking at her like she has no choice, or maybe it's because I'm trembling and looking like I'm barely able to refrain from punching her, but she starts dialing and goes out into the porch to finish the call. Kaiden and I stare at each other in silence before she finally returns.

"He can't get me," she says, and Kaiden is suddenly enraged, turning on her.

"I said get the fuck out. This isn't my fucking problem, you cunt," he snarls with a scowl, and I wonder if he picked her because he saw her laughing at me. If he was doing it to punish her, or me... I didn't even know. She seems shaken by his tone, though, and quickly makes for the door.

"You're fuckin' crazy, Kaiden!" she screams before slamming the door shut. Seconds later, we hear the sound of keys scraping metal. His bike? Or my car?

Either way, Kaiden doesn't budge.

He stares at me intensely, his breathing hard.

"What is it you want from me, Princess? Huh?"

I stare at him, confused bewildered.

"You come here, you fuck up my life, and you take over everything. You come into my home, my job, and my friends. And now you're the one that tells me who I sleep with?"

His voice is this measured calm, this dark, scary tone I've never heard him use before.

Honestly, it's terrifying, and he looks so intense I can barely breathe, let alone answer.

"I can't get you out of my head, and then you start taking over my life too," he growls, and it's like there's a heavy pit in my stomach. I don't want him to go on, I don't want him to keep talking, and I take a step back. But he follows.

The kitchen is small enough that it only takes a couple of steps before he has me pinned to the wall, one hand over my shoulder, glowering down at me.

At six and a half feet tall, he's built like a truck, and I feel so tiny.

"What do I have to do to get you out of here, huh?" he asks, tapping his temple. "I've fucked every broad that comes into that place, and not one of them can get you out. And now I have to see you every goddamned day of my life, prancing around like I'm the scum of the earth, and you're untouchable."

He pauses, but he doesn't stop. His words are slurred and dark, his breath washing over me.

"I got away from you, I got my life back, and then

you come wandering back. Making me *want* you again, and all the while, you act like you're too fucking good for this world. But if you eat with the pigs, Princess, you can't be surprised when you get a bit dirty."

I can't believe what I'm hearing, and my heart is pounding so loud that maybe I'm hearing it all wrong.

Is he saying that he feels for me the same way I feel for him?

I stare up at him, and he leans closer, his mouth approaching mine. I can smell the whiskey on his breath, and I want, more than anything, to simply silence all my fears on his lips. To just succumb to what I want so fucking bad.

His green eyes caress my face, his tongue runs along his upper lip as he leans in further. He's only an inch away, and I want him. My stomach clenches with desire and I need him so fucking bad.

Instead, I run.

don't know where I'm going. I just need to get away from him, from what he said. From how it made me feel.

The road is so dark, I can barely see anything, even with my lights on. Not a soul around.

I'm completely and utterly alone, and the sensation is at once comforting yet so alienating.

Kaiden's words ring through my ears, the way he was staring at me so intently. With such longing.

'*Making me want you again...*'

I had to have misunderstood. It just couldn't be real. I didn't understand how it could be.

It's one thing for me to think about my step-brother like this, but for the feelings to be mutual? That's just me dreaming, wanting for something that can't ever, ever be.

I have to get out. Out of this town, out of this

state, somewhere as far from him and the bar and Ryder as I can get.

I drive for what feels like such a long time but must have been only forty-five minutes.

The sky's turning that navy color, sunrise just an hour or two away, and my eyes are grainy. I can barely keep them open, all the adrenaline of the day taking its toll on me now.

I have no idea where I am, but when I see a sign for a motel coming up, it seems my prayers are about to be answered.

Pulling into a parking spot near the road and walking into the dimly lit lobby, I feel like a zombie, and the front desk clerk doesn't seem much better. Her face is sour and tight, but all I want is a bed for the night, to crash. To be alone and try to make sense of what's happening.

"One night, please," I say, struggling to smile.

"I'm sorry, we're full," she says in return, not even bothering to look.

"But the sign says vacancy?" I press, more angrily than I intend.

I can't believe my luck.

She shrugs. "We're full."

"You've gotta be shitting me!"

The glare she gives me says it all, and I'm too tired to fight, too tired to even cry. A tremble goes through me, and I suck in some breath before simply turning and making my way back to my car.

I can't go on. I crawl into the back seat, pull the itchy spare blanket over my shoulders, and just try to find some peace.

It reminds me of those dark days after losing our home, back when I still had too much pride to talk to Kaiden about it, and I shiver despite the warmth of the night. I just need some sleep, and then I can figure it all out tomorrow.

I WAKE UP STARTLED to a knocking on the window. At first I'm not entirely sure where I am. It comes back to me, slowly.

I slept in the car again.

For a second, I picture Kaiden coming to find me, an extra blanket and a warm coffee in hand, and I smile.

Until I see the early morning light spilling over the cop at my window, lights flashing on his car parked not far away.

"Fuck," I curse to myself, bolting up. My legs are cramped, and I have a kink in my neck, but I roll down the window.

"Is there something wrong, officer?" I ask before I see the desk clerk standing not far away, a smug look on her rancid little face.

"I'm going to need you to step outside the vehicle, miss."

* * *

"KAIDEN... I know you're probably mad at me, but if you get this, I really need your help. I'm at a police station in Ramona, and if you don't pick me up, if someone doesn't pick me up, I'm going to be transferred somewhere else. I don't really know where. They impounded my car..."

I try not to sob as I'm leaving him the message, but I've *never* been in trouble before. Never even been sent to the principal's office. But now I'm in jail, being threatened with some half-baked vagrancy charge. I'd tried to explain over and over that the motel was full and I just needed to sleep, that it wasn't safe for me to drive, but they just kept telling me to tell it to the judge.

I hang up the phone and get escorted back to my cell. It's a gross grey-green color, not really like what I've seen on TV. I guess because it's just lockup and not jail-jail. I go to the table and sit at one of the chairs, listening to the sound of the person in the bed retching something awful.

And all I can do is push my palms to my eyes and sob.

"Please, Kaiden," I whimper under my breath. "Please come."

"Who's Kaiden?"

I startle, wiping my eyes of their tears and try to look... what? Hard? I'm an eighteen-year-old girl that looks more like a high school cheerleader, not a thug.

I look into the face of a woman double my age at least, who's leaning on her knee in the dark corner of the top bunk. I hadn't realized that there were three of us in here.

"My brother," I say too quickly, opening up too fast. I've seen the TV shows, I know these people aren't on my side. But I'm so scared, and I want so badly for someone to tell me it'll be okay, and she looks like she's been here before.

"I'm sorry for, uh, waking you," I say as I wipe the rest of my eyes.

"Don't worry about it, kid. Missy-moo beneath me here is what's keeping me up. Ever since they got rid of the drunk tank, this place has gone downhill." She gives me a wry sort of smile, half-cunning, half-genuineness. She reminds me of one of the customers at the bar. Someone that time and life hasn't been kind to.

But I guess we're both in lockup, so maybe life hasn't been kind to either of us.

"Oh, yeah," I reply, as if I know, but she must be able to see me better than I can see her.

"Your hands are shaking. First time here?"

I look down at my hands before pressing my palms to the table. "Yeah," I murmur, honesty spilling from my lips once more.

She hops down from the bed, away from the

puddle beneath our roommate's face, and joins me at the table.

"What're you in for?"

"Vagrancy," I reply with a sneer, another sob striking my chest. "I just... I ran away, and the motel was full, so I was just sleeping in my car in the parking lot. I didn't know there was anything wrong with it!"

Her mouth goes into a line, the remnants of her lip liner still visible. Watery blue eyes and light colored lashes peer at me. "That's a tough break, kid."

"Why, what are you here for?"

She shrugs as if it's nothing. "Solicitation." She pauses, then continues without needing to, "Prostitution, I mean."

I look away. "Oh." My nose crinkles before I force my eyes back to hers. "Is this... is it your first time for that?"

She shakes her head and looks, for a second, so sad.

"Third time's a charm, right sweetheart?" she says, and my heart breaks for her. I don't know the charges or the sentence she's facing, but I can't imagine it's going to be lenient.

"I'm sorry," I murmur gently.

She shakes her head and gives me a flimsy smile. "It happens. But when you're desperate, you take risks you wouldn't otherwise," she says as she raises her chin towards me. "So what has you on the run?"

"My brother..."

"The same one that you're begging to come get you?"

I laugh, the sound pathetic and soft. "Yup."

Her face is instantly hard, and she leans in, talking more quietly. "Has he hurt you? Laid hands on you?"

I shake my head, feeling a little sick to my stomach that anyone could ever think that about Kaiden. Despite all his hardness, despite all the things he's done over the years, he's never hurt me. Not like that.

I don't even know why it bothers me so much that this stranger would think that, but it does. I feel the instant need to defend him.

"No, no. He's... I mean, he's my step-brother, and I've been living with him for a few weeks, and we just don't... we don't get along that great."

"Your step-brother?" The woman looked at me with a raised brow before she simply shrugged her shoulders. "Well, family's complicated, ya? Why don't you get along?"

I sit back in my chair, and I'll be honest... I'm totally and utterly stumped as to what to tell her. I mean, I know why we don't get along, now more than ever. I know we've been pushing one another away, that we've been trying to deny this... feeling hanging between us. That we'd been needing to put time and distance and space between us, and it hasn't worked.

So how do I tell that to a woman? To a stranger? I just don't know, and I lick my lips. She's just a random person. Maybe... maybe it wouldn't be so bad just to tell her. It's not like I'm ever going to see her again, not once I get released.

"I... we want to be something to one another that we just... can't be." The words feel funny on my tongue, but it's like this sense of relief washed over me. All my anger and rage at Kaiden, all these emotions, they simply started to calm as the weight of the words lingered in the air.

"I see," she says, tapping her fingers on the table. I don't know if it's a nervous habit or if she's just lost in thought—her expression is unreadable. "What do you two wanna be then, huh?"

I swallow, and I can't meet her eyes anymore. I'm too scared of what might be reflected back at me.

"Something...more." I manage. Something so much more. I want to be his. I want to be one of those women that he makes moan and cry his name. I want to feel my body wrapped around him, lost to his muscles, lost to his mouth.

I want to feel his hard body pressing up against mine as he claims me for my own. I shake my head free of the thoughts. It's not an appropriate time for fantasizing about him, to say the least. But at least the thoughts take me away from the jail for a few seconds.

When I look at her again, I see how intensely she's been staring at me, those clear eyes looking through to my soul. It sends a shiver down my spine, and I just give her an apologetic smile.

"Sorry, I shouldn't be talking about this," I say and she shakes her head.

"It's not so bad, being in love," she assures me, and my heart's racing. I'd never thought of it like that. I've always denied that that was the word for what I feel.

But the way it strikes me, I know she's right.

I love Kaiden.

* * *

MY CELLMATE IS STILL dry heaving and shaking like mad on the bottom bunk. I guess she's drying out. They haven't woken at all in the hours I've been locked up in this grungy cell.

Sarah, the prostitute on the top bunk, has finally managed to get some sleep, though she makes these soft little whimpering sounds that make me want to reach out and comfort her. She didn't tell me much about herself, and less about what got her in here, but those pained gasps of her nightmares tell me more than she ever needed to.

I'm still at the table when I hear some noise from

outside my cell. I haven't slept since the catnap in the car, but I'm too afraid to sleep. And, I'm still in a daze about my realization with Kaiden. About what I want from him.

"Abigail Tuney? Someone's come for you," the cop says through the little barred window. "You're being released."

I stand, pushing the chair away and turning towards the door as it swings open. I wonder if I should say goodbye to Sarah, but she's still deep in sleep, and I don't want to disturb her.

My hair's a mess, my muscles all ache, my makeup must be completely smeared or gone and I feel like a mess.

But when I see Kaiden's face?

He looks proud.

And I've never been so happy to see him in my life.

It's been a few days, and things have kind of returned to normal.

Well, I say returned to normal, but Kaiden and I haven't spoken since I got off his bike and went back into the house. I don't know what to say to him, either. I just keep thinking about what he told me...

What I had realized about how I felt.

It reminds me of the time I fell out of the boat. The way he looked at me like he was just seconds from kissing me, and then went suddenly cold out of nowhere. He didn't speak to me for so long I thought I'd done something wrong.

But this time, I'm just as angry at him as I am at myself. Angry at how much I still want him.

He hasn't brought any other women home, either. He's just been locked up in his bedroom by himself, barely eating, though he helped me get my car back from impound at least. Even at work, he's been avoiding me, and part of me is happy for the space.

But a huge part of me is upset that he's avoiding me. I know I started it, but I just want... something more than this.

It's dumb, I know that. But I don't care. If he really feels that way for me, he should do something about it. But of course he won't. I know I won't. It's too risky.

Even if we weren't siblings, just getting closer to him would give Ryder more ammo.

I'm grateful that I have today off. My first day off in seventeen days, and I'm feeling pretty good about it all, other than the fact that apparently Kaiden took the night off too.

I can hear him in his room, the TV on low, but it doesn't matter. The walls are so thin I can still make out every word.

Sounds like he's watching some biker show, random shootouts happening every once in a while and a whole lot of yelling and fighting.

I listen to it for a while, letting my mind drift back to when I was sixteen or so.

I was at home, watching a movie on TV. I was all alone, had the house to myself, so it must've been summer.

It was some crime drama or something, and I remember getting really into it when suddenly someone had their hands over my eyes. I screamed bloody murder, jumped out of my skin.

And instantly, Kaiden apologized.

Big, hulking Kaiden came around in front of me, looking so upset that he'd scared me. He came home for a visit, and just wanted to surprise me. I had leapt up, into his arms, and he'd spun me around like I was nothing more than a feather, and we spent the rest of the day cuddled up on the couch just talking about nothing.

A lump formed in my throat. I wanted so bad to get back to that, to just forget all this had ever happened.

To forget that mom and dad had died, that my college money was spent on Kaiden's bail, that I had to live with him and work in a sleazy bar.

Kaiden's TV shuts off, and it must be around four in the morning; we are both pretty much nocturnal now. I hear him shifting, getting comfortable beneath the blankets.

I picture him lying there, one arm strewn over his forehead as he stares up at the ceiling, bare-chested as the sheets gather around his waist. It's still warm out and we don't have air conditioning, so I imagine his leg strewn over the blankets, barely clinging to modesty as he closes his eyes.

And then I tap, softly, on the wall.

It is barely more than a touch of my knuckle to the drywall, but I know he heard it.

He simply doesn't respond.

"Kaiden, you remember that time when I was fourteen, and I was supposed to have that birthday party? It was going to be princess-themed, remember? Mom bought all those pink decorations, plates and balloons and streamers, had them up everywhere. I was so excited, I just couldn't wait. I'd invited all my friends on these little themed cards, and told you that you had to go and that I didn't want you there. I was just so embarrassed to have my big brother hanging out with my friends, stealing all their attention."

I pause, but he doesn't say anything, so I continue.

"But then... my friends all just... didn't show up," I say, my voice strained and I can feel tears burning at my eyes. "They all had just decided that princess parties were too young, not cool enough for them, and they never told me. So I was just sitting there in my dress, waiting for them all day. Mom kept telling me to come inside, to just open presents with the family, but I was in disbelief that they'd stand me up. That they'd be so mean."

The pain still feels so raw. I had been so humiliated, so hurt. They'd told me the day before, promised me they were going to come.

"And I was crying on the steps when you came home from being with your friends. You were skateboarding back then, remember? And a lot skinnier, but I think you'd already gotten your first tattoo and your tongue pierced, and you always had that stupid mohawk," I say with a bit of a laugh. "When you found out what happened, you were so mad, and I remember you ran inside, right to dad's closet and grabbed one of his suits. It didn't really fit, but you smoothed out your hair, and you offered me your hand, and introduced yourself as Prince Charming. Mom and dad put on some music, and you made me dance with you until I stopped crying and started laughing."

I smile at the memory, remembering his young, punk rock phase and how hard he always looked, but for me, it was nothing but affection.

He still hasn't said a word, though, and I worry he doesn't remember, or doesn't care. It makes my heart hurt, and a tear spills down from the corner of my eye.

He was my hero back then.

He was my everything.

But after that party, I started having feelings for him. Feelings I shouldn't have, and I started pushing him away. Little bits at first, and then when he turned eighteen and moved to a different town, it was easier to forget all of it and pretend like it was nothing but a girly phase. I dated, tried to move on and have my own life. But now here I am, back under the same roof as him, and my feelings are burning stronger than ever, even with my anger.

I swallow back the lump in my throat, the hot air

feeling so heavy on my chest, and I push down my blanket, my nightgown already damp with sweat.

It's minutes later when I finally hear him, his dark, rumbling voice penetrating the wall.

"I remember, Princess."

That nickname again, this time said with such tenderness instead of scorn and mockery. I sob again and try to quiet it, trying to fight the urge to break down. I can't handle him hearing me like that.

"I miss them so much."

"I know…" There's a brief pause. "Even though I hadn't seen them in a while, I still expect to go home and find them there, like nothing has changed."

I don't know what to say to that, because even though I know they're not there, part of my mind tricks me into thinking I just haven't seen them in a while. As if they're not really gone, they're just not around.

The thought breaks my heart, and I push it away.

"I miss you. You always looked out for me, even though you never had to," I whimper, my voice pathetic.

"I tried."

He's still being short with me, but at least he's talking. That makes me feel a little better, and I imagine opening my door, going to his room, curling up with him. Feeling his skin against mine. Just like we had on the couch all those times. I don't even know what part of him I'm craving. The part of him that makes me feel like he's my hero, that he'll always protect me? Or the part of him that makes women lose their minds, willing to give up so much just for a chance to sleep with him?

I shudder at the thought, because deep down, I know I want both. I want him, wholly and utterly.

"When did things get so... fucked up," I say softly, my body sticky, and my sex throbbing with heat. The tension between us is driving me mad in more than one way, and his words keep echoing in my mind. The intensity in which he had said them.

"I don't know, Abby," he says with a deep gravel to his tone, sleeplessness getting to him too.

"Was it the drugs?"

"Naw... that was just a side effect."

"Then why? Why'd you move away?"

There's a long pause, and I'm afraid he won't answer. Lord knows I'd asked him that question enough over the years, and never got one. The clock in the kitchen ticks past the seconds, the sound echoing through the quiet of his house. I start drifting between sleep and wakefulness.

"I didn't want to hurt you."

His voice makes my eyes flutter back open, and I wonder if I heard him right. "You hurt me more by leaving," I croak in return, that lump in my throat making it hard to even speak.

Another long silence spreads out between us, and again I want to go into his room, to see his face. But it's easier like this in some ways, not knowing.

I lick my lips.

"You never even told me you got arrested. Mom and dad, they never told me..."

"I asked them not to," he says quickly. "I didn't want to worry you, Abby. You didn't need that on your plate, not with college coming up."

"But they spent all my college money on that. On your bail, and it still hasn't gone to trial?"

"It's not fast and they've been delaying it. And I didn't know mom and dad... I didn't know they were in so deep. I never would've asked otherwise, but I didn't want to owe that asshole anything more than I had to."

Was he talking about Ryder?

A chill went through me, and my anger gave way to exhaustion.

I close my eyes, breathing deeply as we both drift to sleep.

KAIDEN

"We're going to get this done, Ryder. This is the last fucking bit of your shit I'm moving, and after that, I'm done. No more threats, no more fucking with Abigail. She gets fired; that's it."

Ryder is giving me the smuggest fucking smile, and I feel like pummeling it off his pretty boy face. He looks like a movie star, but he's colder than any man I've ever met.

I sneer at him, folding my arms across my chest.

"This is it, Ryder, do you understand? You let this thing go to trial, you get me off, and you let her go if I do this for you."

"Sure," he says in that way that makes me instinctively not trust him.

But I don't have a choice.

There's only one way I can deserve Abigail, and

69

that's if I get clean of this mess I got into trying to run from her. From how she makes me feel. No woman should ever make me feel like she does, and I've fucked dozens of them trying to prove that to myself, and my thoughts always go back to her.

Abigail.

From the way she tugs on her hair when she's angry to the way she always frowns at her reflection right before going out. Everything about her just gets in under my skin, and when I saw how she looked at me the other night... I was going to lose my mind if I didn't at least see if she felt the same for me.

Even if it meant running drugs with some of the worst people I've met.

"Fine. Tonight, you do this thing for me, and you and your little sister," he says, waving in the air, "can go. But if you fuck up? She's the one that's going to pay."

"Drinks, shots?" I'm trying my best to treat this like a normal night, but I have a bad feeling in my stomach.

I woke up excited to see Kaiden this morning, but he was already gone.

No note, no text, no nothing.

And my instinct is to worry that I scared him off again and put more distance between us.

I give one of the men at the table his whiskey and cola, glancing around the bar. No sight of Kaiden, but honestly, that wasn't unusual. I'm just being paranoid.

I move to the next table, handing them their drink before going back to the bar. It's a slow night, and I'm getting exhausted fast.

I refill my shot glasses, putting others in the dishwasher when I realize I forgot my phone in my purse. I curse and, with a quick apology to the bartender, run back into the office. It's pitch black, but I always put my bag in the same place. I find it and turn it on, hoping for a text from Kaiden, but there's nothing.

I sigh, and then I hear the shifting of a chair. Gasping, I look up to see Ryder approaching me slowly. I didn't even know he was working tonight. He usually takes off before midnight.

"Sorry, Ryder, I just needed to check my phone."

He tut-tuts.

"Checking your phone on work hours? I didn't take you for such a bad girl," he says, and through the light of my phone, I can see him leering at me.

I remember back to my first day when I met him, liking the way he looked at me. His gorgeous face, his strong, masculine form... it was hard not to be attracted to him.

But now all I feel is fear, and I think he can kind of sense it. Especially when he reaches out and touches some of my hair, his hand grazing along the shell of my ear.

I flinch away and his smile widens.

"But I bet you *are* a bad girl, aren't you? I see you, prancing in here with your short skirts, your low-cut tops, just begging for it," he says, his hand running down my neck. I'm too scared to even move, though I'm desperately trying to force my legs to run, to get me away from him.

For Kaiden to come in and save me.

Anything.

His smile is feral, and I can smell his cologne in the air as he leans in, tucking hair behind my ear and whispering in it:

"I bet you like it up the ass, huh? Prissy girl like you already looks like she's got somethin' stuck up there."

He grabs my wrist, and I try to yank it away, only for him to put more force into it. Making my hand touch against his bulge, his hand moving overtop mine and making me feel it throb against my touch. I pull away, but he pins me to the wall with his body, his scent overwhelming me.

And then it's all over. He pulls back and returns to his desk as if nothing happened, clicking on the desk lamp once again.

"Get the fuck outta here, girl, you got a shift to finish."

I didn't have to be told twice.

I ran out the door, back into the dingy club and the oppressive music. My skin is burning with heat and anger, fear almost crippling me. But I can't tell the bartender what happened, so I grab my tray and simply go back to work.

Kaiden, where are you?

KAIDEN

I have a really bad feeling about this. Already the guys I'm supposed to meet are running fifteen minutes late. I've dealt with a lot of bullshit over the years running drugs for Ryder, and I know that when someone's late it's because they're getting cold feet. And the only reason someone truly involved with this business gets cold feet is because they're planning on screwing you over.

I sit back in the seat, looking at the guy next to me. He's shorter and scrawnier, looks like a junkie, but I know he isn't because Ryder won't hire a junkie. Too big of a risk of losing product.

His name's Mustang or something stupid like that, but I've worked with him a couple times before and he's surprisingly sharp.

We're in the middle of nowhere, but I recommended the spot. I don't know why, but when we were kids, Abigail's dad and my mom took us here. I guess it was just to show us a life outside of suburbia. We spent days going from small town to small town, talking to people, spending the night in "mom & pop" motels.

And then we went camping, out in the middle of nowhere, just us and the stars. We purposefully tried to find a place that was just far enough away from anything that we could feel really alone.

A bonding exercise, mom called it.

Abigail and I shared a tent, stayed up so late just listening to the little night critters come out and scuttle around, telling each other ghost stories and giggling until mom and dad had enough and threatened to take us back to the city.

I look back at the desert, over the utter darkness that sprawls out in all directions and let my stomach and heart turn to steel. This is for her, I remind myself. If I can do this one thing for her, just get us out of this place...

I don't have time to finish my thoughts. There's headlights in the distance, probably a few miles away, heading towards us. I nudge Mustang. He gets out of the van, and I follow, my hand on my gun.

I check my phone again, feeling terrified.

Ryder's words, the cold way he'd said them... I want out, but how can I leave without Kaiden getting in shit?

I'm in so far over my head, and I keep fucking up drink orders, which I never do. I'm a perfectionist, even at this, but I just don't have my head together. I give another apologetic smile to one of my regulars — Ryan. Every day he orders a rum and coke. So why did I bring him a whiskey?

My hands are shaking as I take the drink back, but he's looking at me with concern. He's probably forty or so, I guess, and even after a couple of drinks is nothing but a gentleman, which is more than I can say for anyone else here.

"You alright, darling?" he asks with none of the

aggression of most of my clients, and I give him a half smile.

"Yea, sorry. I'll go fix your drink," I apologize, but he reaches out before I can and lightly grabs my hand.

"C'mon now, Abigail. I ain't never seen you less than chipper, even when that guy laid hands on you. You always come back like nothin's the matter, so this gotta be serious," he says, his voice lowered.

I hate it when people can see right through me.

Sometimes I just wear my emotions too clearly, but he's right. Here? I've been able to suck it all up and just hide it, but not tonight. I'm really, genuinely worried. I just have this feeling in my stomach like something is very, very wrong.

I bite on my lower lip, shaking my head.

"It's nothing. I just haven't seen Kaiden lately and usually he's here by now." How stupid do I sound? Most customers know my relationship with Kaiden isn't great and even a ton of non-regulars have seen us fight more than a couple times. Ryan has definitely seen more than his fair share of our screaming matches, despite his insistence that I'm always chipper.

I take a deep breath and shake my head before looking back at Ryan and giving him an apologetic half smile.

But then I see something in his eyes. Something that confirms everything I dread.

My shoulders slump.

"Oh my God, what's wrong? What's happened?" I ask, and my blood turns to ice. He can't be dead. I suck in air, my heart racing as panic grips me, and Ryan's hand tightens around mine.

"He's had to work out some things with Ryder in the desert," he says, and the apologetic tone...

Ryder's going to kill him!

I glance up at the bar just in time to see the golden hair of Ryder making his way past the crowd to the door, pushing out. Seconds later I hear the rev of his bike, and I pull away from Ryan.

I don't have any control over my actions as I run out the door, jumping into my car.

I have to save him!

* * *

I know this road.

Just a hazy, faded memory of being down here before, past the strange, colorful mansion, recessed away and lit with blue floodlights. It looks just as I remember it, and the memory of playing a stupid car game fills me.

"I spy, with my little eye, something that is green!"

"Come on, Abby! That's so easy. There's nothin' green out here 'cept that house," Kaiden says, punching me in the arm. We're too old for these games, but we've been

driving forever and we're both getting bored out of our minds.

"Fine, fine. I spy, with my little eye, something that is purple."

Kaiden looks around, trying to figure it out in vain, and I feel really smug that he can't see it. But then he spots it in the distance, a weird little lighthouse mailbox, painted purple, and he points at it with a grin.

I pass off the same mailbox, and I know where Ryder's going. This was the way we drove when we went camping that time, so many years ago.

In the middle of the desert, so far from everything...

Dread grips my heart. Ryder's way off in the distance, and I have my lights turned off. I know how dangerous it is, but getting Ryder's attention is way more dangerous, and the road is abandoned this time of night anyways. There's not even any street lights illuminating the way, and the sound of Ryder's bike booms loudly.

I try to keep up while keeping far enough away that I won't be seen, my hands shaking and I grip the wheel tighter, trying to calm my nerves. He's going to be fine. This is Kaiden. Big, strong, tough Kaiden.

My hero, Kaiden.

My love, Kaiden.

The thought comes to me unbidden, and yet I know just how true it is.

Beneath all our fighting and arguing burns real

passion that I've been hiding from for so long. All the anger I've felt towards him, all the resentment, it all stems from him leaving me. From the fact that I can't get him out of my life.

The realization is intense, and for a moment, thoughts of Kaiden fill my mind. Smiling at me after I give some sassy comment and the way he touched his hand along my jaw and looked at me right before he left home. Even the anger when he saw me on his doorstep, begging for a place to sleep now brings a pitter-patter to my heart.

And just as I'm lost to my pleasant reverie, Ryder's bike turns off the path. I'm too far away to see exactly where he's going, and I start getting panicked until I can see off in the distance a set of headlights.

I open my glove box, grabbing the gun my dad gave me for my birthday last year. In case of emergencies only, is what he'd said, and this was definitely an emergency.

I park, my lights still off, and get out of my car as quietly as I can.

In the desert, sound travels differently, and I take each step as quietly as I can, my high heels left behind in the car, the warmth of the day still radiating upon my bare feet. When we were kids camping out here, we used to listen to the little animals walking around, so I know I have to be delicate.

My eyes adjust to the darkness, my heart racing as I walk, trying to avoid the few sources of lights. I can see at least two vans and Ryder's bike, probably a quarter mile in the distance, and I move faster.

"You think you can threaten me?"

The words reach me and send a shiver down my spine. Ryder.

"You think *you* have *anything* over me?" He's screaming now, but I can't quite make them out. They're behind one of the vans. I start running.

"You need to be reminded of your place, fuck-head. You are nothing without me. I took you and molded you into a fucking man and you think you can turn your back on me? You think you can tell me what you're going to do, just because that cunt of a sister walks back into your life?"

I'm close now, just a few feet away, and I crouch down. I can't move to see them without getting in the light of the vans, so I lay flat on my belly, looking under the van at their feet.

There's four of them. And all of them are facing Kaiden.

"We had a deal, man! What will Axel say?" Kaiden protests, his voice low and angry, and Ryder laughs.

"Ah yeah, our 'deal' where I leave your little sister out of this and get you out of your jail time and everyone lives happily ever after? Not going to fucking happen, and Axel will be none the wiser. You went down in a bad deal."

Ryder's voice mutates into one of sick cheer that turns my blood cold, "But, Kaiden, my boy. Don't worry. We do have a *very* special guest here tonight, so you two can die and rot together."

He knows I'm here.

KAIDEN

bigail is here.

My hands clench into fists, and I stare at Ryder, my green eyes locked on his steely blue gaze. I can't believe what a fucking scumbag he is, and he's the guy that wants me to take the fall for him.

My lips turn into a sneer, but I don't move an inch. I have to bide my time, let him think he's won.

"Why're you doin' this, man?" I glare, my arms loose and at my sides, ready for a fight. "I already fuckin' agreed to do everything you wanted, and it still wasn't enough."

"Because, asshole. I knew you were gonna try somethin' funny. Guys like you can't be trusted," Ryder said, taking a step closer to me, his gun still in his hand.

It's me facing off against four thugs, and I have to think fast.

Where's Abigail? She'll have her car, but we're going to need to get to it, which means we're going to have to run, and we have four guys with guns waiting for us to make a move. They'd love to just shoot us in the backs.

"I wasn't gonna fuck you over, Ryder. I've been here this whole fuckin' time just waitin' for the day I had to go down for you, to pay my dues, but you won't even give me that? Three fuckin' years I was lookin' at, and I stayed here the whole time, just waiting for it, and now you're saying you didn't *trust* me? Why didn't you just kill me back then, huh? Why hold this over me 'til now? I could've fuckin' talked at any point and I kept my fucking mouth shut, just like you wanted."

Ryder's eyes narrow and he paces just a foot in front of my face, hands on his hips, gun at his side.

"You wanna know why I didn't kill you, you punk piece of shit? Because you mean nothing to me. Less than nothing. You were just some lost little kid and I took you in as the fall guy, but now you've got your sights on bigger things, huh? Don't think I haven't noticed how protective *big brother* is."

He smirks, and I've never seen him look so scary.

So cruel.

And I've seen him kill a man. I know that glint in his eyes, the way he was drawing out the moment, savoring it.

"So now, the game has changed, hasn't it? You have a reason to stay out, and put me away, is that what you think?" He turns, putting the gun square to my chest and though I try not to show it, I feel like my heart has just stopped and my life's flashing before my eyes. He cocks the pistol, his blue eyes hard and cold.

It's not like it was the last time he had me at gunpoint, asking me if I was gonna narc. That was just a test.

This is serious.

But instead, he laughs, and the thugs at his sides don't know what to make of it. They shift, uncomfortably, as they watch their boss and me.

"You've never been nothin' but a little fuckin' punk that thinks he's got his shit together when you are nothing. *Nothing*, Kaiden. You hear me?"

He removes the gun from my chest, nodding at Mustang. "Get the girl."

I see the boots move towards me, and I try to crawl in further beneath the van. My eyes are blurry and I'm trying desperately not to cry because I can't see and I need to be able to move and think quickly.

We're a long way from my car, and I swear, I just heard a gun get ready to shoot.

But when the guy moves towards me, I think fast, pushing my gun in towards the front tire of the van. I hide it from view, hopefully getting it close enough so that Kaiden can get it.

But how will he know it's there? I won't be able to tell him...

There's not enough time to think about it. Someone grabs my ankle, and I kick, but he's strong. It only takes him a second to grip me and tug me from under the van.

I'm still in my work clothes, but I'd taken off my heels to walk, leaving me in a slutty miniskirt and a flimsy top, dirt covering my skin. I scream and kick at the man, trying to struggle free, but it's no use. He's too strong, and he grabs me by the waist, tossing me over his shoulder as if I weigh nothing.

Seconds later I'm tossed down to the dirt again, right near the front of the van, the five of them surrounding me. Kaiden tries to move to my side, but Ryder holds the gun on him again and he freezes.

Ryder nods to the man that carried me over and suddenly there's a gun on me too.

"You thought this was gonna be you getting out, boy?" Ryder hisses, his voice filled with rage. "It's you getting out, you and your little sister, but you're goin' on a one way trip to hell," he says with a scowl. "Any last words?"

Kaiden's breathing hard, and I can see his face is red from out of my bleary eyes, and he's looking at me with such sadness it's breaking my heart. He looks so sorry, so fucking sorry, and I just want to hug him and tell him it'll all be alright.

"Yea," he says, his voice softer than I've heard it in so long. "Abby, I never meant to get you into this. Never. I always just wanted to protect you," he says and Ryder laughs, cruelly, as I'm shaking with emotion. "I love you, Princess, you get me?"

I nod, and the gun at my head cocks and all I can see is my imminent death.

"I love you too!" I practically screech, my body shaking in the dirt as I cringe away from the gun.

My eyes are shut and I prepare for the end, our whole miserable lives set to come to a close, and I can feel this deep, dark pit in my stomach. And at the same time a weight lift off my shoulders. It was a strange, inexplicable feeling that I'm not sure I'll ever understand.

The gun goes off… but I'm still alive.

I look, and there's Kaiden. He's slugged Ryder and he's coming for me. It's a brief moment of glory, my brother charging in to save me, be my hero once more! I could cry, if I wasn't already bleary-eyed and in a panic. But it's all for naught.

One of the other guys cracks Kaiden in the head, and then the guy pointing his gun at me pulls the hammer back with a click. Kaiden comes to a stop, fearful for my life, and once again… it's all over.

I can only watch as my brother is laid into, two guys pounding on him in vengeance for his outburst.

"You're gonna fuckin' watch her die, prick! But not before we make you pay for that lil' show," says the guy over me, who moves over just enough to strike out with a kick into Kaiden's side. And it's like I can feel every blow that lands upon my big brother, twinges of guilt and sympathy pain wracking my body.

I can't wallow in the pity for long, though because I notice that the man's hold of the gun has wavered. He's watching Kaiden now, not me, and the gun I left beneath that van is so very close…

I can rush for it, but I remember something I heard on TV long ago: the human eye picks up on fast motion far quicker than the slow. So instead, I'm cautious, and though it hurts me to do so, I let Kaiden take a few more punches and blows. A cracked rib too, by the sound of that crunch, and I'm so damn sorry for him.

But it's better than having no chance at all.

My hand reaches beneath the vehicle, searching through the sand and dirt for the feel of my gun. For a moment I worry that I'd placed it too far out of reach, but then… oh yes, the cold press of steel to my fingers and palm.

I've got it!

I pull it out, slowly, slowly… *don't rush Abigail, don't blow it*. I raise the weapon, point it at the man over me— the only man still holding his gun at the ready then— and squeeze the trigger.

The kick on the gun comes as a surprise, even though it shouldn't. I know what to expect, my father taught me, but I'd never fired at a human before, and maybe that's what really gives it the kick. I pull the trigger on him, then I point at the other guys.

"Leave him alone!" I scream, my voice sounding

manic, insane! I'm nearly out of my mind at this point, watching Kaiden being beaten, knowing that they might've done serious harm to him already, or worse.

And while my threat got them to still, the guy I just shot wasn't out of the picture.

The shot was near point—blank, but I didn't kill him. Not even close. My bullet struck his shoulder, maybe only grazed it, and while blood gushed, he wasn't going down. He'd dropped his gun since I'd wounded the arm that held it up, but that didn't stop him from hitting me with the other fist, and my world spun from the rough blow.

"Kill that fuckin' bitch," came Ryder's cruel voice, sounding tired of the whole affair.

We had been so close, and now it's all over. I close my eyes, waiting for the sound, but where I fell, my big brother came to pick me up.

In the brief moments of my almost-glory, he got up. His fist sent a spray of red from the one man's face as he took the handgun from him, a mere moment later and two shots rang out. One man was definitely dead, or just as well as.

Kaiden is like a wild animal; he'd become a force of nature itself, and with a fury and rage that surpasses any I'd seen, he lets loose a roar and comes for me.

Comes to my rescue.

He strikes down that piece of shit, putting

another bullet in him, then another. Kaiden isn't taking risks, not like I did. Sympathy only put us both in danger, and he'd learned from my flash-in-the-pan attempt to rescue us both.

I scramble for my gun in the dark, but Kaiden, oh Kaiden… he's wrath incarnate. He's standing up, tall and strong, gun pointed at the once cocky Ryder.

"You shit, you think this is ov—" Ryder's cocky words are silenced by the pull of Kaiden's trigger. The boom of the gun shot drops the man, and the insufferable asshole is down on his back, clutching his wounded neck and screaming in agony.

Kaiden advances on him, gun still aimed for his head. And he pulls the trigger again.

"No Kaiden!" I cry, but it clicks. And no boom follows.

It clicks again, then again.

"You don't fucking touch my sister!" Kaiden shouts, leaning to one side as the gun is now useless, but his body is still sore and smarting from his beating. Instead of a bullet, he plants the heel of his boot into Ryder's face.

I don't know where we are or how long we've been driving. It's still night, but even without the streetlights, I can see the pain etched on Kaiden's face. Blood is caked beneath his nose, and he's holding his side. His shirt is torn in a few places, and I know I should be more concerned, but honestly...

That was the hottest thing I've ever seen in my life.

It's always been a constant thing with us. It's not the first time he's kicked someone else's ass for me, but it might be the first time he's been beat while doing it. I shake my head. I know the thoughts are inappropriate, in more ways than one, and I just try to focus on the road. It's so quiet, but I don't feel safe being anywhere near Ryder.

"We need to take you to a hospital," I say, but I

don't glance at him. I know a hospital is the last place he'd want to be after a fight like that. I'm pretty sure one of the conditions of his bail would be that he can't be involved with those people or alcohol or whatever anymore.

"I'll be fine," he instantly replies, though he winces a little. "I just need a place to lay low. We should be far enough away, but if you see an all-night pharmacy..."

He trails off, and I nod obediently.

"Just rest back," I say, adrenaline still coursing through me and making me more lead-footed than usual.

Mile after mile of road spreads out, California desert on all sides as I make my way west, towards our old town. It's not that I want to go home, but I just don't know where else to go, and I'm craving the comfortable, the familiar. All I have on me is a hundred bucks in tips, and instinctively, I know there's no going back to our trailer.

Ryder'll have people looking for us, and I glance at Kaiden.

His eyes are shut, and though his lips are still pulled into a sneer, he's absolutely gorgeous. Everything about him, even in his pain, just screams out for me.

I lick my lips, my heart beating so loudly in my chest.

"You saved my life," I murmur, not even sure if

he'll hear me. The words hang between us, and I drink the entire situation in, trying to cope with what just happened. I have no idea what Ryder is capable of, but now I do, and I don't know what to do next.

"Right back at you, Princess," he says in his gravelly husk of a voice, so raw and harsh after the night we just had. "If you hadn't given me the distraction, it's likely they would've just put me down on the spot before I had a chance to turn the tables."

He winces again, his thick, muscular arm draped over his battered side as he sits there beside me in pain. He'd taken a brutal beating from four big, strong guys and still has it in him to turn things around and save us both. This is a miracle, all things considered, and judging by the fact that I heard a crack or two, he has at least one broken rib beneath his bloodstained shirt.

I stare ahead, desperate to keep my mind off of just how damn attracted I am to him right now. We've spent so many years running from one another, running from our desires and God only knows what else.

And look at all the good that's done us?

He's facing prison time, and we're both on the run from a killer.

"We can head back, go home," I say distantly, but he shakes his head with a groan.

"No need."

I look at him, my brows furrowed.

"I knew what I was getting into, Princess, and that I likely wouldn't be coming back. I transferred all the money I had saved over the years into a safety deposit box in your name."

"My name?" I ask, drawing in my lower lip, and he nods.

It's not just the pain of the beating getting to him.

"I've done some stupid things in my life, Abby, but I saved every penny. I couldn't tell anyone about it, I couldn't pay my bail with it because I didn't get it legally. So mom and dad went broke, and I was just sittin' on money I couldn't spend. So a few months ago, I set up some safety deposit boxes in your name."

I can't believe what I'm hearing.

There's a part of me that's so mad, so outraged that maybe there was a way mom and dad didn't have to sell out my future to bail him out. But it's tempered with gratitude.

"How much?"

He swallows with a wince and his breathing is a bit off, but he looks at me and rests his hand on top of mine.

"When I transferred it, there was $1.5 million."

I must have heard that wrong.

I slow down for a second before I remember we're on the run and speed up once more.

"Over one *million* dollars?"

He smirks, proud of my surprise, but he looks like a scolded pup at the same time. He won't meet my eyes, and he nods more seriously.

"Kaiden, what the fuck? How did you get over one million dollars?"

"Working for Ryder, doing odd jobs on the side... taking the fall for him. He wasn't happy about that last one and I knew he'd try something eventually. Then I invested it in some other projects a guy I know out of state was involved in, before taking everything out and putting it in your name, Princess."

I don't know what he expected my reaction to be, but I'm dizzy and disoriented, and have to blink to clear my eyes.

"You'll have to be careful with what you do with it, I mean... no matter how this all goes down, it's still suspicious money. You gotta be smart. But hey, I know I can count on you to be smart. Always could," he says, smiling just a little at memories past, even as he sits there in such obvious pain.

He'd taken down all those thugs, nearly killed Ryder too, though once that was done, it was as if I watched the steam come out of him. He had deflated before my eyes, and staggered, nearly falling over before I could get to him and help him into my car.

I'm in shock, and I nearly miss a familiar sight. It's a little motel, recessed into the trees, but the neon lights are still on. I remember the name vaguely, and I point to it as I start slowing down.

"Kaiden, I remember this place. When the house was being fumigated that time, we stayed here a few nights, remember?"

Kaiden looks where I point, his thick, strong neck no longer supporting his head so sturdily thanks to the beating.

"Of course I do," he rasps to me, so damn tired and weary. "Mom and dad left us to our own devices most of the time there, and we broke into the manager's office. Found all those porn mags and liquor stashed in his desk," he remarks with a dry, brief laugh. "We could be such little shits. But hey, we never got caught. And that's what really matters," he adds jokingly.

I laugh, biting down on my lower lip as I pull in, parking the car out of sight of the road. I'd completely forgotten that. He had a habit of bringing out the rebel in me, making me want to misbehave.

He still does.

I open my door and come around to his side, leaning in the open window.

"Stay here 'til I get us a room, no need to draw more attention to ourselves than needed." Of course, with my torn tank top and dirty mini skirt, that's going to be easier said than done anyways.

He looks me over, and even in his wounded, pain-racked state, he manages to crook a brow and look interested. "Dressed like that, Princess... I don't think you can avoid drawing at least half the world's attention. But you're right I guess. Best we leave it at just half if we can help it," he prods me back, reaching out and pinching my side through the tear in my top.

A week ago—hell, a day ago—I would've flipped at him. Let my fear of falling for him make me push him away again.

But I'm too exhausted, and he looks too good for me to keep it up. Maybe it's just that I'm running on instinct, that adrenaline is still pumping through me, that I nearly died, but I just don't care anymore about pushing my emotions down.

I bite down on my lower lip, tugging it into my mouth as I stare at him, my heart skipping a beat before I take a step backward. Quickly I turn to make my way to the front desk, but the entire time, my mind is stuck on him.

I look around, and even in the darkness, I can see how little the motel has changed. It's aged a bit over the years, but it's quiet and surrounded by trees and privacy. I make my way into the office, ringing the little bell before trying to fix my hair in the reflection of the window.

"You need a room?" comes a bored voice, and suddenly I'm reminded of the last motel I was at and what a mess that became.

I turn and smile at the young man, and nod.

"Okay, we have a double bed available just next door," he says, taking the key off the hook board and I pause.

"What about two singles?"

My heart is instantly racing, and my stomach lurches though I don't know if it's out of fear or excitement.

He shakes his head.

"Just the one double. There's a school group in," he replies, and my heart beats faster, my body feeling suddenly warm.

"So it's just the one room, nothing else?"

"Right. You want it?"

I head back to the car, keys clutched in my hand.

Kaiden looks like he's passed out, and I rush over to him. But before I can even reach out and shake his shoulder, his eyes open and he looks to me.

"Don't tell me we're sleepin' in the car. As I recall, that didn't work out so well for you last time," he remarks with a wry smile. He sees me dangling the keys and pushes the door open to get out.

"They only have the one room," I say as I try to help him out, "but they have a vending machine in the lobby with some Tylenol and water."

I feel hot and uncomfortable, though, and the thought of sleeping with him in the same bed is messing with my mind.

He looks down at me as we make our way to the room.

"There's something else you're keeping from me?" It's half-accusation, half-question.

I hate that he can tell, and I just shrug, trying to look nonchalant.

"Just the one bed is all."

He's looking down at me, brow arched in silent questioning as we reach the door.

"I dunno if either of us is in much shape for sleeping on a floor tonight," he says. He's still holding his side as he leans against the door and I work the old-fashioned keys in the door. "And as old school as this place is, they might take issue with us livin' in sin like that." He has a big grin on his broad, handsome— but battered— face.

I roll my eyes, but I have no idea how to feel about it as I push the door open and take in the familiar smell. It's like I'm taken back five years, and I'm just a kid again. But I flick on the light and help Kaiden to the bed and I'm reminded of just how much I'm not.

"Stay here, I'm going to grab you some Tylenol," I say before making my way out once more and to the machine. I'm grateful for the time away, but honestly, all I can think about is coming back to him.

Spending the night with him.

It's so wrong, picturing his body pressed to mine, the way it makes my knees tremble with desire and my hands shake with uncertainty. Maybe I should just spend the night in the car, get away from it all and then just... take off.

But I know I can't. We're in this together now, and I'm not going to run from it.

When I return to the room with the Tylenol and water, though, and see him shirtless, laying back on the bed, I can't help but stare.

His broad chest exposed, thick, corded muscles all on display as he rubs at his body, testing his ribs, clearly checking to see if any were broken. He's bruised, badly so, and cut in a few places, but none of that ruins just how much sex appeal my he has as he lays there, inspecting himself.

"Luckily, none of those idiots were clever enough to buy a pair of steel-toed boots," he says. Judging by the grimace he gives as he presses along one rib, though, they'd done one hell of a job without it anyhow.

I go into the bathroom, grabbing a towel before returning to him, kneeling on the bed.

"Here," I say, passing him some pills and the bottle of water as I bring the slightly wetted towel to the bow of his lip, cleaning him of the blood from his nose.

The motel is completely silent, and I know it's probably just before dawn. There's that strange stillness in the air, like all the world has fallen away. Everyone but Kaiden and I, holed up in a motel room at the edge of town.

"We should really go to a hospital," I say with a whisper, my hand reaching out, trembling before I lightly touch my fingers to the bruise along his side. He winces, and I withdraw my hand, but I continue to stare.

"You know we can't do that," he says, his bare chest heaving with his heavy breathing. He's a massive man, and so battered and bruised, he looks like he's a gladiator from out of the past, having come to save me when I needed him most.

He lets me clean his wounds with the wet towel, knocking back the pills and water after I move from his face, on down to his bloodied torso. Though all the while, his eyes are upon me no less intently than mine are on him.

"Whatever happens, I don't want you to be in any more trouble, Princess. You hear me? That money is sittin' and waiting for you, and whatever comes, I need you to be safe, so I know you'll be able to enjoy it. That means more to me than anything right now," he says, his husky voice so rough and firm.

When I don't respond fast enough for him, pondering his words and what they meant, he reaches out, grasps my arm and squeezes. His bicep bulging as he does.

"You hear me, Princess?" he says, but his words aren't angry, they're… loving.

My eyes flit to his, and I nod gently, though I

have that sick feeling in my stomach and I know I'm not going to run this time.

More importantly, I'm not going to let him run.

I hold his green, smoldering gaze and swallow.

There's always been this strange emotion, this connection, and we've both tried so hard to ignore it. It wouldn't be bad just to ignore it one more night. Just fall asleep, like we were kids sharing a bed.

I sit back, putting the towel aside before taking off my high heels and letting them drop to the floor.

"We'll figure it out tomorrow."

Though how I would keep my calm next to my girlhood crush, when he's lying there, glistening and bare-chested, looking gloriously tough after putting his life on the line for us both…

He doesn't quite let go of my arm though, and no sooner are the heels off than he tugs me in. I land upon his lap, where he clearly intended me, and he pays no heed to the pain that must've caused on his battered form.

"I don't think I've ever had so clear a view of what to do in my head than right now, Abby," he says, his voice deeper, darker. Filled with lusty desire that made him into a man that was irresistible to all the ladies.

Me included.

"I saw my life flash before my eyes back there," he says, continuing on as he looks over my face before resting his gaze back to mine. "And my only regret… was not letting you know how much you meant to me. How much… how much I fuckin' wanted you in my life. In every way."

I pause there, in part because I'm afraid of hurting him, and in part because I'm simply stunned by his words. There've been hints, clues, little subtle things that I kept thinking were all in my head, but now…

Now there's no denying it.

Staring up at him, I swallow, and my lower lip trembles as his hand moves from my hand, running up my forearm, then my bicep, then up to my jaw, forcing my gaze to not falter from his.

"I know it's wrong, dammit," he curses, the words so raw and unhindered, spilling out after long being kept in check. "And you can pull away at any time and I'll stop… pretend none of this ever happened, if you will, Princess. But… fuck it."

That was that. He had lost his patience for words, and simply pressed in, pushing his lips to mine and kissing me hard and deep. His eyes shut as our mouths melded, his tongue sliding between the seams of my lips and beyond, despite the groan of pain he couldn't suppress.

I'd thought about it for so long, daydreams and fantasies alike all centered on those lips meeting mine, yet the reality of it could never have compared to those thoughts. Of how firm his lips are yet how soft and yielding they are against mine, how insistent he is. My breath is short, and I can barely contain myself as his tongue caresses mine.

My better judgment tells me to do just what he offered. Pull away. Stop it. Stop him. This is *wrong*.

But I can't. There's a shy, hesitant moan that escapes me, and no matter how wrong it is, I've wanted him for so long...

Kaiden pulls me in closer against him, all the bruises and battered bones be damned, he wants me pressed in against his flesh and that's what he takes. And I can feel him... so lewdly pressed beneath me, that manhood which had pleasured so many women just a couple of feet from me through the walls between our rooms... it was now not even an inch away.

Separated only by his dusty jeans.

Our lips smack, and he wraps both arms around me, resting his hard, strong hand upon my thigh running up to my hip as he squeezes and rubs at me. He's insatiable for me, and his every motion speaks to that. There's no longer any hiding just how deep the well of his emotions run.

They run at least as deep as my own.

And the fact that I don't pull away, that I don't run, that speaks volumes and only encourages his motions.

Most of my clothes are torn, my miniskirt barely covering my ass, my tank top stretched and loose. I feel dirty, sore, and yet I don't care about any of that.

Instead I push back against him, my hand going to his shoulder as I rub him.

I can't believe it's finally happening. It's so surreal, but if it's a dream, I don't want to wake up.

Those strong fingers of his slide up along my thigh, in underneath my skirt to grasp at my bare cheek to the side of my panties. My shame is cast aside by him as he kisses me deeply and feels my body.

It isn't long before he pushes me over, onto my back atop the bed as he comes with me. His big, broad form looming large as he kisses me, feels me.

Appreciates my every inch.

It's like a testament to how great his desire for me is, and how strong he is, that his powerful body holds itself up over me with all feelings of pain pushed aside. Forgotten.

And with it went all the cultural taboos. The fact that we both know this is forbidden, if not legally, then socially. The fact that we both know we're off-limits to one another.

The fact that that's what's kept us apart for so long.

But with his heavy, muscular body weighing down on me, I've never felt more right. Despite the fact that I'm a virgin, that I've never gone further than a little touching with a guy, and had heard him screw so many women, that was what got me the most.

If there's anyone in the world I wanted to give my virginity, though, it's him.

I knew he would understand my body better than even I could, judging by the many pleasured sounds I heard each night for so long. And I knew, beyond all shadow of a doubt, that he would look out for me.

His actions tonight prove it.

Kaiden squeezes my ass cheek, then slides his two hands up my side. He takes hold of my flimsy tank top, the garment already ripped, and pulls it up over my head to grasp at my breasts. His fingers sink into the flesh over the top of my bra, and though I was tiny—oh so tiny compared to the women he went with!—he revels in my breasts as if they were the most sumptuous tits he's ever felt.

A low, husky growl rumbles out of his broad, barrel chest, and I can feel his dick throb through his jeans so excitedly.

Throbbing, hard for me.

It almost makes me sick, that rolling pit in my stomach growing.

I shouldn't be doing this.

I shouldn't be kissing my step-brother, and I definitely shouldn't be getting so wet at the fact that he's got an erection over me. That he's squeezing my breasts, and making my body sing.

But I've never been more turned on in my life, and I can't hide the little moan that escapes my lips, or the way my body rolls into his hands, begging for more as my legs spread. I want him so bad, no matter how wrong it is.

I've never made love before, but with Kaiden—despite all my reservations about how taboo it is—it feels more natural than drinking water. It's like the absolute perfect outcome, tailor-made for me.

His every touch, his every kiss, so satisfying, intensifying. I'm putty in his hands, and he's taking full advantage of that, undoing my bra, squeezing at my chest as it returns to its almost flat state, undeterred by it.

Even knowing all the gorgeous women he's been with, he makes me feel like I'm the best. The most beautiful. The one he desires most. I believe it, despite all of my own inhibitions and self-doubts.

Those full lips of his move down from mine, smacking noisily across my neck, along my collarbone. Until at last, he's at my breasts, kissing in around my pink areola, skirting their edge as he moves ever closer, circling around until the first touch upon my tender tits makes me gasp and squirm.

I glance down when I can, but my eyes keep fluttering closed, my body jolting against his as his tongue teases one of my nipples to hardness. He runs the flat of his wet muscle along it before sucking it into his lips. I gasp, sucking in breath, my pussy throbbing with need and desire.

All logic has fled me, all sense of right and wrong. Instead it's just me and Kaiden, giving in to what we've tried to hide from for so long.

My legs wrap around his hips, and I grind against his stomach, though it does nothing to quell my need, just fueling my passion higher.

"Oh God," I gasp as his teeth lightly clamp around my nipple, tugging it gently and lighting a spark of excitement in my loins.

He's big, he's strong, he's a rough guy with a rough past, but he handles me with such care. Teasing me with his rough edges, but never hurting me.

It's intoxicating, to be held in his arms, under his power, laying all trust in him as he squeezes, rubs, bites and suckles at me. Counting on Kaiden to lust for me, ravage me, but not go too far with my delicate, untouched body.

He tugs at my nipple, suckling it before letting it snap back into place. His big hands slide down my sides, reaching in beneath my skirt. Instead of pulling my panties away though, he begins to gently rub his thumb over the fabric, along my slit... feeling the warmth and wetness there, rubbing my most sensitive of areas as he continues to tease and provoke my body to new heights.

I shouldn't be doing this. There's no way that I

can survive this, go back to just being normal with him. Not after getting what I've been wanting and looking for for so long.

Years of fantasies and daydreams couldn't have prepared me for the reality. Not even listening to him as he'd take another woman just inches from my head could've made me realize what it would actually be like when I'm in his arms.

He touches me, ignites such a need, and I press in against his fingers, hoping and praying that he won't stop even as I will myself to just... what? Push him away? Put an end to all this, to put us back right where we were all those years, fighting our desires? To lose him all over again?

I'd been without him for so long, tried to push these feelings from my mind, but they didn't go anywhere. They just remained, lingering in my sub-conscious, begging for me to just give in to passion, to give in to my needs.

To give into our forbidden lusts.

"Oh God," I whimper into the air of the motel, my head tilting back, my body aching for him. "Kaiden!"

He pulls away from me, releasing my breast, my pussy, and I fear he's going to think better of this whole, ill-conceived infatuation we have for one another. But he looks me in the eyes as he breaks my leg lock, and moves on down my body.

Kaiden's gaze stays with mine until he's prying

my thighs open wide, then looking down at my covered slit.

I'd heard him take so many women, but I felt so very special under his care. He strokes my soft inner thighs, then leans in.

Inhaling my scent, a shudder passes through him before he leans in, kissing my pussy through the fabric of my panties. Even with that fabric between us, it feels so… so intense. I can't quite get over how much intimacy is compacted in that one press of our lips.

Then, as I'm still lost in excitement, he tugs my panties aside, and I'm aware that the one man who shouldn't be is staring at my bare, glistening pussy. And he loves it. Kisses it. Tastes it.

Tastes me.

His tongue ring grazes against my clit and I jump. I've fantasized for so long about what that hard little piece of metal would feel like, and the contrast between his soft, wet tongue, and that firm piercing is... surreal.

But even more than that is the fact that this is Kaiden.

I lift my head, look at him between my pale thighs, and I feel so dizzy with lust that I'm afraid I'm going to pass out. He looks so fucking good, so serious, and I'm quivering with such need.

I'm soaking wet, I know that. It's not the first time Kaiden's gotten me wet, even if it is the first time that he's done anything about it. And I wonder how often he got hard thinking of me.

Thinking of what he'd do to me.

What he *wanted* to do with me.

My breathing is like little pants of breath, and I try not to moan, but I fail. Even when I bite down on my lower lip, I'm still not able to hold those sounds of pleasure in, and I shift closer to him, my entire body affected by a tremor.

"You feel so good," I gasp, clutching the blanket. "I've never... never felt like this."

He doesn't respond. At least, not with words.

Kaiden's response is physical and intense.

He grasps my two thighs, sinking his thumbs into my soft inner flesh and keeping me pinned to the bed as he works his tongue over my pussy aggressively. All I can see is his dark hair, his broad shoulders with their bulging muscles, but what I feel is explosive.

Each pass of his studded tongue around my pussy is more than I can handle, yet they're not alone. One stroke after another, he lashes his tongue over my slit, making me feel pleasure like I'd never even dreamed of!

And how could I conceive of such sensations when I had nothing to go on?

All of my fantasies have been so... shallow compared to what he's making me feel now, and I cry out, arching my back and body. I want to get away, to escape the intensity of the bliss he's giving me, and yet he doesn't let me. He keeps me pinned in his hulking arms, holding me to his mouth and devouring me hungrily.

He's like a wild beast, a savage, making me almost cry from how good it feels. How much I've wanted this for so long, and it was always just a pale glimmer of this moment.

"I... oh God!" I gasp. I want to confess, for him to know all my sins, all the horrible thoughts I've had about him, all the desirous things I've done. All the times I touched myself thinking of him, or listening to him as he fucked another woman, wishing it were me.

I just don't have the power to speak any longer.

He's giving me so much, but he also takes from me my ability to speak in whole sentences.

That tongue, that devilish tongue, continues to lash and swirl when one of his hands releases my thigh. And though I clamp my leg immediately against the side of his head, I couldn't disturb his work. He is a rock, immovable. Even as a pained growl runs from him to me.

Instead, he goes about his business, sliding his long index finger deep into my slick, wet pussy. The tip of his digit parting my folds, tracing around them, teasing and circling, until it sinks in and stretches me around his finger as he gives me my first feeling of being full of him.

It's only a finger, but with the work of his tongue, it adds to the intensity of my pleasure so well.

So wrong. So very, very wrong.

I'm being finger-fucked and eaten out by Kaiden.

I swallow, and there's a pit in my stomach, but it feels so amazing. I don't want him to stop, not even for a second, even as I try to squirm away. I'm breathing so hard, and all rational thought has left me.

All I want is him. His hands, his tongue, his cock.

Oh God, his cock.

I haven't even seen it, and only felt its hardness through his jeans, but the thought of him actually really fucking me, combined with the ministrations of his tongue and his finger sends me over an edge. I scream, filling the shitty motel room with the sound of my explosive pleasure.

I buck against his face and he holds me right where he needs me as he suckles upon my clit, making that intense high even better.

I scream until I'm red in the face, my entire body bucking and protesting, needing a reprieve from his skilled tongue. From how those waves keep crashing down on me, threatening to take me under and submerse me utterly in bliss.

Kaiden gives me my break, but on his own time, at his own pace.

A few final smacks of his lips resound as he

kisses my pussy, then rises up to lick at his mouth and savor my flavor.

There he is again, and though my sight is blurry after my intense climax, I can see that gorgeous man. He's stunning. Battered and bruised, with muscles bulging, he's the most masculine man I've ever met, and I adore that about him

I lust for him as much as any woman could lust for a man.

It's pure torture as he reaches down past his bulging abs, slowly undoing his jeans, peeling them down to show the bulge of his black boxer-briefs.

That bulge.

It's immense!

It looks even bigger than it felt through his thick cotton jeans. A large snake that extends out to his hip, pulsating beneath the dark fabric.

My imagining of what it must look like doesn't last much longer though, because he peels the underwear away too, and out it comes…

That thick, veiny girth, bulging and pulsating with such intense desire. It's obscene! It's utterly and completely obscene. I shouldn't be looking at this! And yet my breath is stolen away by it.

The purple crown is glistening from pre-cum and his heavy sac dangles beneath as he slides out of his clothes entirely and returns to rubbing his hard, strong hands over my legs.

"Dammit Princess," he says, as if still trying to

restrain himself. But he's failing. Miserably. Endorphins must be rushing through his body, distracting him from his pain, because other than a wince here and there, he looks like the picture of power.

He wants me so bad, and we've already reached the point of no return. This time, I'm not running. This time, I'm not going to try to fight what's happening, not again. I want him too bad. I want him to take my virginity, to be the first man inside my body.

I look down at his cock, my breath short and my throat hurting from all the screaming I've done.

"Kaiden," I gasp out, my voice sounding so different than what I'm used to. "I've never been with anyone," I say, though I know I don't have to. Maybe I shouldn't have. Maybe he'll change his mind, leave me here wanting and needy for him.

The thought terrifies me, and I sit up, moving towards him as if I'm in a trance. Like the sight of his cock is drawing me in, making me reach out. I touch my slender digits to his shaft, running them along the pulsing surface.

It's gorgeous.

He's gorgeous.

I lick my lips as I look up at him, scared about what he'd do or say next.

As my fingers touch upon him though, his eyes descend, nearly shutting.

If my words got through to him, he doesn't show

it. He's too enraptured with my touches, my skin upon his most private and sensitive of flesh. And the lewd bulging of his manhood against my palm is so… prominent. So dirty.

He's trying to resist, I know that. And for a moment I'm panicking that he'll do it. That he'll end this all here, even if that's what part of me says I should want. That I should want him to have the strength to run when I don't.

But he doesn't.

Kaiden reaches out, grasps me by the shoulders and lowers me back down onto the bed, his mouth burying itself into my neck as he presses upon me once more.

I realize he's too far gone to go back now, just like me, and we're barreling over that precipice together, completely.

There's no going back, not after this, but I don't care. I moan as his mouth caresses my throat, as his body grinds against mine.

"Oh Kaiden," I whimper, his tongue caressing the delicate skin along my throat, nuzzling my hair out of the way.

Tonight we nearly died together, and now, it's like we both started finally embracing life and what we really wanted rather than denying ourselves that thing which we needed.

"Kaiden," I gasp again, his teeth nipping me just a little, just enough to send a jolt through me. "I want you to be my first. I need..." I say, but my words are cut off by another moan.

His strong hands slide up and down along my sides, he's squeezing my breast in one hand, my hip in the other. It's such a beautiful feeling to be manhandled by my Kaiden, knowing he wants me so very, very bad.

"Abby," he murmurs into my ear in between nips of my sensitive neck, his words so deep and dark. "I've never been with a woman without usin' a condom. Never," he husks, kissing me again.

"I want us both to have a first," he growls before biting me, pushing his hips forward so that his thick cock prods at my tiny pussy, his tip sliding along the slick lips.

It's totally and completely irrational what those words do to me.

There's no other explanation but irrationality that my hips lift towards him and I press myself against that flared tip. There's no other explanation for the way a tremor goes up and down my spine, little fireworks of pleasure starting in my clit and moving up through my torso, excited jolts traveling through me.

My eyes flutter closed and my lips drop open as I grind against him with no other reason or desire than just to feel his body against mine more fully.

I know we should both just stop before it goes

too far, but the thought of him taking me, raw... of my being his first...

I can't deny the desire that draws up in me.

"I want you so bad," I gasp. "I've wanted you... thought about you... for so long."

His hand at my hip reaches out, fingers sinking into my ass cheek as he grasps and gropes at my body. He's ravenous for me, and I can see it in his emerald eyes.

"You're the only woman I've wanted to fuck... the only woman I've fantasized about fucking, for so... so damn long, Princess," he says, his voice deep and gravelly with desire as he nudges in against me. "Every fucking one of those women I brought home, I was only thinking of you." That thick crown of his manhood spreading my pussy lips just a little, making me flower around him as he gives a low groan that resonates out of his chest.

It's slow, but it's sure: he's taking me.

My first time has already begun, and I can feel his dick sliding into me, stretching me out and deflowering me as that big, muscular man shuddered from his own joy at the act.

"Fuck Abby," he groans.

He's so big, but I'm so wet, and that helps a little. Though he's still spreading me open so much wider than I've ever been, and I cry out, a little bit of pain mixing with the amazing sensation of his spreading me open.

In all my fantasies, I never knew it could feel like this, and my hands grip the cheap sheets as he impales me.

He feels so hot, so thick, and I can feel the beating of his heart through his huge tool. Every pulse resonates through me, and for the first time, we're really, truly linked.

My arms go around his neck, holding him close to me, drawing him in as he kisses my forehead, soothes my pain.

"That's it, Princess," he growls, his voice both sweet and hard, complementary and lust-ridden as he steals my virginity.

His one hand grasps the bed, bunching it up in his fingers as he squares off his shoulders. He's straining himself, doing his best to ease me into it after my confession.

But his need to satiate that thick cock inside my pussy is too much even for him, and he doesn't stop, doesn't stall. He sinks on down until he's reached my utmost depths, and I can feel the incessant throb of his manhood.

Again and again it's stretching my pussy walls, bulging and pulsating, turning my narrow little virginal pussy into a sleeve for his cock.

His eyes are shut tight, but I can hear his gravelly moan as he shudders. All those powerful muscles, able to withstand a savage beating and still come to my rescue, brought to bear by the pleasures of my body.

It made me feel drunk on sex.

"Fuck, Abby…" he growls out, tugging back on his hips, so that my clinging pussy pulled against him. "You're perfect," he breathes out, slowly starting to fuck me upon that cheap motel bed.

It's not how I would've anticipated losing my virginity. In some tawdry room to my high school crush... To my step-brother.

But I can't think of how it could be any more perfect.

We are finally, blissfully one.

We've been fighting it for so long, and now my legs are wrapped around his waist as he fucks me. He's bruised and broken, but still, he wants me.

Needs me.

My mouth goes to his and I kiss him, deep and hungrily, needing to feel and taste and smell him so badly. I've never been so turned on, and so happy.

My tongue caresses his, running along his stud, my fingers digging into his back. I know his body must still ache, but he doesn't let it show. His craving for me won't let him.

So as his powerful body picks up its pace, hammering down into me with blow after blow of his thrusting shaft, he appears godlike and unbeatable. None of the cuts or bruises of the night faze him.

Though all that is inconsequential, because I'm just lost to the bliss of his cock plowing into me. Again and again it fills me up and spreads me open, making me feel so incredibly full. So desired. So wanted. Needed.

Those husky moans, so masculine, yet conveying the weakness of his desire for me.

He squeezes my breast, forces his eyes open to look down upon me, soak in the sight of my body rocked by his pumping thrusts. To gaze at the lewd sight of my pink little pussy spread wide and filled with his shaft, again and again.

My body is still tingling with my orgasm, and every strike of his body against mine takes me closer to that brink again. Closer to the point of absolute and utter bliss.

I want to hide from it, not to cross that line with him, but there are no more lines. It's all just blurred together into wrongness, into wonderfully unbridled lust.

"Oh God, Kaiden," I gasp, my hips tilted towards him, letting him sink into me so deep. "I've dreamed about this..."

His hand slides down to my hip, up across my thigh, and he lifts it up, taking my leg over his own hip. He plunges down into me oh so deep, and I catch glimpses of his ripped physique undulating as he fucks me in the fog of my pleasure-blurred mind.

"Ohh Princess... you feel better... better than I

imagined," he pants out in his deep, dark voice. "Better than any of those women I tried to fill the void of wanting you with."

He's so sincere, and I can feel his dick throbbing wildly as he takes me.

His pace is quickening, and I can hear the bed groan and creak beneath us as he fucks me harder, faster. The loud sound of his balls slapping against my ass resounding throughout the room.

I arch my back, and there's no turning back. There's no denying my body its pleasure as it washes over me. It's softer at first, but then it starts to build at a pace I'd never experienced before. Every thrust takes me higher and higher until a scream comes from my lips and I clutch onto him for dear life.

My fingers and nails sink into his hard, muscled flesh, but he doesn't mind.

He couldn't.

He pummels me with his dick as he too goes spiraling out of control. His cock swelling, so stiff and hard, as his balls tighten and he's fighting his urge to come.

It's a losing battle though, as I clench around him in my moment of intense pleasure.

I'm flailing, writhing, and he's the only thing keeping me in place. Grounding me through the point of our loins where our bodies are firmly marked as one.

"I'm cumming, Princess," he roars out like some giant beast, and I can feel it.

I can actually feel his thick, massive cock reaching its potential.

His muscles bulge and as I'm lost to a sea of pleasure, he joins me.

"Take it, baby," he growls before all words are lost and he's just shooting his thick, creamy load deep inside of me. Spurt after spurt of that rich, creamy come filling my every crevice.

I cry out, his words teasing me to a new high as I grind into him, gasping and sputtering and losing my mind.

And then we're left panting in one another's arms, holding on to one another as we're spent and exhausted, his cock still pulsing within me.

I lay still, afraid if I move, I might break the moment. That any breath I take might make this spell disappear and we'd be brought back to reality.

Kaiden's not so sheepish, though.

As weary and beaten as he is, he has it in him to reach out, pull me into his big arms as he rolls to his side. Our bodies are still interlocked in that smooth movement, and I'm pressed against his glistening torso, a thin sheen of perspiration highlighting the contours of his bulging muscles.

Though words he has few to spare, he merely cradles me in his strong grasp, strokes my hair and kisses my forehead.

For how lewd and raunchy it was to fuck my own brother, he makes the aftermath sweet. Caring.

I curl into him, grateful for the quiet. For him leaving me to my own thoughts. It's not that I don't want to understand what just happened, what it meant for us, for our future.

It's just that for now, I need the opportunity to bask in feeling good for a few minutes.

My eyes close part way and I can feel his heart still racing in his chest. He's so warm, his body pressed into mine, and I've never felt so at peace.

Morning comes too soon. I unravel myself from Kaiden's body, my skin clammy and chilly at the same time. My clothes are still in a pile on the floor, and for a moment, I feel sick. I look over at his bruised and battered form, listen to his raspy breathing and remember what we've done.

It's wrong.

I push myself out of bed, grabbing at my clothes and throwing on the torn and dirty garments. Sunlight filters into the room through the cheap curtains, illuminating my Kaiden's body in this almost ethereal light, his gorgeous form practically glowing. I find myself staring again, my stomach churning in disgust and fear.

What have I done?

I gave in to the one thing I know I shouldn't have,

and I swallow hard before moving to the washroom. My stomach churns and a wave of nausea washes over me. I hug the toilet, heaving into it, but nothing comes out. My hands tremble against the cold porcelain, the dirty floor biting into my knees.

Slowly the sensation passes, and the rest of the night begins filtering back to my consciousness.

I just made love to the one person in the world I should've resisted, after almost being killed by a gang, and now we're on the run. How could my life get any more messed up?

I shiver as I look into the mirror, seeing my messy, blonde hair, my dirty clothes.

That little bit of excitement lurking between my eyes. Despite it all, despite everything that had happened, losing my virginity to Kaiden was the best part of my life. It was... amazing, and I can see that hidden smile, the goosebumps that run up and down my arms.

I wanted him for so long, and his body was made for me.

It's perfect.

But what now? Do we go back to pretending this never happened? Or just run off with the money, find somewhere safe and comfortable and just be together?

I want it so badly to be the last one, despite how much that scares me.

"Abby?" His voice is hoarse and he sounds even

more hurt than he did last night, so I hurriedly splash some water on my face before returning to the bedroom, giving him a weak, nervous smile.

What's he going to say?

Is he going to freak out? Panic? Regret everything like I'd been fearing we would?

But his expression warms as he sees me and he relaxes back into the bed, his hard bicep bulging beneath his arm.

"Hey, Princess," he says and the words roll off his tongue so seductively.

I want to go over there and curl up against his nude body.

There's only the cheap, flimsy blanket covering him, and even through that I can see the regular throbbing of his cock. His eyes work up over my body, over my bare thighs, my half-exposed breasts, and I've never felt so desperate for more.

I go over to him, reaching down and touching his forehead.

"Do you need more water?" I ask, but I can't tear my gaze away from his bare chest.

It wasn't that I'd never seen it before, he was always strutting around shirtless. It's just that now I know how it feels pressed against me, the sensation of his warm weight down upon me.

His hand goes to my waist, drawing me in, and I topple down against his body, and he pins me there in one hand as he grinds his erection against my thigh.

"I need something else," he husks, and despite his bruises now turning an ugly purple, he has strength to spare for me. He reaches beneath my skirt with his free hand as his mouth goes to my neck, and suddenly I'm putty in his hands. There's no stopping him as he strips me of my panties, the scent of last night still hanging in the air.

Next he pulls away the blankets, revealing that gorgeous cock of his once more, standing tall and thick, throbbing with need as he tugs me atop him.

I straddle his waist, my mind in a daze as he guides my motions. And when he presses that flared tip to my sex, I tremble with desire and need.

"I want to see you," he says, though part of me wonders if he's just in too much pain.

Either way, though, I look down at him with the filtered daylight spilling over his body and feel so naked and exposed despite still wearing my skirt, bra and tank top. He's watching me, licking his lips as his hips grind subtly.

He doesn't push in, not yet, just teasing my wet seam as we stare at each other.

I wonder what he's thinking, and when I let myself drop along his cock, feeling him spread me so wide, I watch his face. Hesitation gives way to bliss, his eyes fluttering closed as his hips rise to meet mine, pushing himself in deep until he's lodged all the way into my pussy.

We don't even have the excuse of adrenaline, of the nighttime and the strange daze that comes with it. Here we are, fucking in the mid-morning, so wantonly.

And it feels good.

I hurriedly strip out of my top and bra, my light pink nipples already so stiff and hard, and instinctually he reaches out to grab one between his fingers, tugging it. I arch my back in pleasure and he groans in kind, our bodies grinding against one another.

He's so damn hard, and so big, and feels so good. I flutter my eyes shut, no longer able to take the fact that he can see my body so clearly that he's watching as I ride him. Instead I just focus on the feel of his body against mine, his fingers and his cock teasing me.

"You're mine, Princess," he growls as he brings his other hand to my clit, rubbing it gently. "And I want you to know you're mine for all time."

I shiver, my pussy already so wet, my entire body calling out for him as I begin to ride his cock, up and down, his hands never leaving mine.

He's able to get so much deeper into me now, and I have to back off a few times as he bucks in, taking me deep into places I've never been before.

Both of his hands move from their positions and

he brings them to my slender hips, feeling over my miniskirt which is little more than a belt now.

"Look at me, Abby," he commands, and I'm helpless to disobey.

He licks his lips, looking so devilish I can barely stand it. He doesn't break our stare as he holds my hips in place, then begins to move them gently. I'm fully impaled on his cock, my heart racing so hard, but the way he's making my body grind against him...

I gasp, my clit pressing against his pelvis and my eyes flutter shut as a wave of pleasure goes through me.

"Eyes," he demands, and I open them again. "I want to see your face while you come on my cock."

Those words turn my body red, my stomach churning, yet they have a very unwanted side effect as well.

His dark, twisted words...

They send a tremor through me, and I begin grinding against him of my own power, one of my hands resting on his chest. Blonde hair spills over my cheeks as I stare at him, his cock firmly lodged in me as I rub my clit against his pubic bone. I'm already so close to cumming, I can feel it, shame and fear and excitement mingling in me.

"You like that, Princess? You like being watched as you come on me? As you feel his cock throb inside you, ready to burst?" His words are like a potent growl, and I moan and whimper, but my hips work faster, my need mounting.

I'm so close. So very close.

"I'm gonna come in you, Princess," he warns, his eyes dipping to my chest, then down to the obscene scene of my pussy wrapped around his thick cock.

He took my virginity not six hours ago, and now he's back for more, and I want it so bad.

"Come in me," I whisper, surprised to hear the words even coming from my mouth!

But oh, I want it so bad, and I rise up off his cock before slamming back down, jolting my entire body, fireworks going off throughout my nerves and my mind. I do it over and over again, impaling myself upon him, the sensation almost painful but in such a good way.

One of his hands goes to my jaw, raising my head, making me look into his beautiful green eyes for a mere moment before they close and his face contorts. His lips screw up at the corner as he tilts his head back, a loud groan emitting from his lips as he holds my hip in place, making me take him as his member expands and fills me with his cream.

I've never felt like I do at this moment, watching Kaiden lose control of himself, of every-thing, inside me. It's not like last night, in the smoky darkness, hidden from the sight of what sin we were doing. Now everything seems so much more real.

I lunge down, kissing his lips hard as my body still writhes in the aftershock of my orgasm.

I still want more, so much more. He's opened the floodgates to my pleasure, and I grind against him full of need.

But after a couple seconds he hisses, grabbing for his rib, and I still, looking down at him with concern.

His lips twist into a smirk and he looks back at me, rubbing my hip between his thumb and his index finger.

"It's nothing," he promises, thrusting his hips up a little as if to prove it to me. "Just in a shit ton of fucking pain."

I smirk, my nose crinkling. Same old Kaiden.

"You can help, though," he says, and I'm nodding before he can even finish his sentence.

"You could get me cleaned up."

I stare at him for a second before standing, watching as his come spills from my pussy, dripping down along his cock.

I leap from the bed to grab him a towel, but before I can even make it a step, his firm hand is wrapped around my wrist and he's tugging me back to him.

"With your mouth, Princess," he says, his eyes flashing, and I can feel heat rising up within me once more.

Oh my God.

I swallow, looking back at the mess of his beautiful cock, and I'm drawn to it. To see what he tastes like. But I feel so exposed, and so dirty. He tugs my wrist again, and I don't have any option other than to crawl back into the bed with him.

And when he knits his other hand into my hair, guiding me down, there's no refusing him.

His motions are forceful, powerful, but they're not cruel. He guides my face to his turgid length, and the scent of him fills my nostrils.

I lean in, kissing the tip of that swollen head, and he groans.

"I've dreamed about seeing you between my thighs, Princess. Licking my cock like a popsicle." My heart was thudding so loudly in my chest I can barely hear him but the flat of my tongue goes to the bottom of his cock, and the salty-sweetness hits me.

I'm licking Kaiden's cock.

"Wrap your lips around it," he commands, and I do, taking him into my mouth as he guides my head. "Savor it. Lick it. Clean me up of the mess you made."

Every time he talks, his filthy words filling the air, my clit throbs and a rush of pleasure goes through me.

"That's it, Princess. Take it all in. Breathe through your nose. Good. Hold your breath." And with that, he forces my head down further, and his cock swells against the back of my throat, cutting off my breath.

He held me there for a few moments, the sounds of pleasure he made so exquisite before he brought me back up.

"You look so good on my dick," he coos, his hips starting to buck a bit more irregularly. He still hasn't softened at all, his cock still hard as a rock, and I grip his thighs tighter for balance.

"I'm gonna take such good care of you. Get some regular fucking in your life, fill you up with my come every fucking night, Princess. That's a promise," he says, his words growing louder, his pain forgotten as I swirl my tongue along the head of his cock.

It feels strange, but so good, and I find myself bobbing atop his cock with greater urgency, with more need, and his hand on the back of my head loosens, letting me go at my own pace.

"Fuck!" he curses, and I can tell he's getting close. That just spurs me on to go a bit faster, my entire body moving as I suck him off.

"Hello?" comes a voice at the door, a man, followed by a knock, and I stop what I'm doing.

Kaiden looks at me, panic in his expression as he moves away from me, grabbing for his jeans. I leap off the bed, grabbing my tank top and tossing it on over my head.

"Who is it?" he hisses, nodding to the peephole, and I make my way over as I tug down my skirt.

Looking out there's a short man with glasses

perched on the end of his nose. He looks annoyed, and he knocks again.

I turn to Kaiden, shrugging, my heart racing as I whisper back, "I don't know them."

We stare at each other for a second before he nods, moving to the bathroom, his gun in hand. He holds a finger over his lips, telling me to be quiet about his presence, and I open the door through the chain lock.

"Hello?" I say softly, my head tilting to the side as I try to smile. I feel like I stink of sex, and my mouth is still raw and wet from my step-brother's cock.

"It's checkout time," he says with some annoyance, tapping his watch, and I sigh in relief.

"Oh, right! Yes, sorry, we're almost done," I say, my cheeks flushed. Could he hear me through the door?

This place is built so cheaply...

"Hurry up," he says before turning and heading towards the next cabin. I shut the door and look at Kaiden, letting out a sigh of relief.

"We gotta go," Kaiden says, grabbing for his shirt and pulling it on.

I know he's right, but I can't help but be disappointed that our tryst was over so quickly.

And when I look at him and see that lust burning beneath his gaze, I know he feels the same.

"Where are we going to go?" I ask behind the steering wheel.

We've barely turned out onto the road, and now I feel lost, faced with our reality once more.

"Ryder's not gonna rest. I only grazed him, it probably looked worse than it really is." Kaiden shakes his head, his breathing a bit raspy. "I never should've let him live."

"You did the right thing, Kaiden. You couldn't just kill a guy. Have that hanging over you?" I shoot him a look. "You'd be facing a lot more than three years in prison for that."

He stills, looking at me with his face contorted in confusion.

"I never told you how much time I was looking at, Abby," he says, and my face goes red. That's because he never told me. I found out when I was eavesdropping on him and Ryder that night at the bar.

I lick my lips nervously, but I know I have to come clean.

We're in this together now, no more secrets.

"I heard you and Ryder talking... fighting... one night. Outside of the bar."

He stared ahead at the highway, clearly trying to remember what was said, and he exhaled, his words dark.

"Oh. Well, then you know what this guy's capable of, Abby. He's not going to stop until he gets his payback, but listen, I have a plan, alright? I'm taking the fall for Ryder's crime anyways. He got caught selling, it got violent. Ryder hid the guns, but best case, he's still looking at trafficking and assault. If we go to the cops, I have enough evidence to take him down. Not just for the crimes he pinned on me."

I glance over at Kaiden, nodding along with his words.

"If you think it'll work, but who's to say Ryder won't just be let out on bail and get payback then? Like, witness protection?"

He shakes his head.

"Naw, the big boss wouldn't let him. He contacted me a couple weeks ago, after you moved in. He wanted me to take Ryder out, to let him take the fall, but... with you here..."

He trails off, and I know where he's going with it.

With me here, Ryder could get his revenge even if he's behind bars because of the big boss. I lick my lips thoughtfully before nodding.

"Alright, so we go to the Sherriff's office, then," I say, and Kaiden gives me a pained smile, his hand reaching out and gripping my knee. "I don't regret it, Abby. I don't regret anything."

I exhale a breath I didn't know I was holding and gave him a sweet smile in return.

There'd been so much messed up stuff happening, but if it led to me being with him, I didn't regret it either.

* * *

"WHY ARE THE COPS HERE?" I ask, squinting along the long stretch of highway.

Kaiden is bothered by the sight of the road block, even as he tries to brush it off.

"Probably just to catch drunk drivers."

"It's eleven in the morning," I say, my nose crinkling, but there's nowhere else to go. Just the highway and a whole lot of more highway. We're only ten minutes outside of town, and my palms are sweaty against the wheel.

"Just act natural, Abby. You'll do fine. Just don't draw any attention to us that we don't want."

I stare at him, and we both know that's going to be impossible. We didn't have time to shower, our clothes still covered in dust and dirt, torn and ripped in places, and his black eye is, well... it's hard not to miss.

I slow the vehicle as we get to the traffic stop, putting on the brakes as we approach the first officer.

"Is there a problem with the road?" I ask, trying to be as sweet as possible. The man is likely only five years older than me, still a bit baby-faced, and he glances to his superior.

"Abigail Tuney?" he asks, trying to make his voice sound deep and commanding, but he doesn't have to. The fact that he knows my name sends a chill up my spine.

My stomach lurches, and I look at Kaiden desperately, but he looks just as surprised as me.

"Y-yes?" I say, terror beginning to grip me in earnest.

Are we arrested? Did Ryder already go to the cops and tell them what we did? We still have the gun on us! Damn it!

Not like ditching it would have been any better, since it's registered in my name.

"I need you to come with us."

"But... where?" I'm trembling, my hands slick on the steering wheel, and I'm trying not to hyper-ventilate.

"We need you to just come with us." He reaches for the driver's door, pulling it open, and I undo my seatbelt. "Kaiden, you too," he adds on, and Kaiden's already getting out of the car, his hands on the roof, his legs spread.

Another officer goes and frisks him, finding the empty gun in the low of his back, and I'm shaking so bad I can barely walk. The officer wraps his hand around my upper arm, guiding me to the cop car.

"What about my car?" I ask, my voice high pitched, and he gives me a brief look of pity.

"It'll be taken care of."

The officer guides the two of us back to the back of the cop car, though neither of us are handcuffed. That part stands out to me as really strange as we start heading down the road into town, but Kaiden's staring out the window, aloof.

It scares me that he's not looking at me, not reassuring me, and my stomach churns.

I feel like I'm going to be sick, my mouth watering, and I swallow it down nervously.

It's not long before we're pulling up outside not the police station, but a grungy warehouse that I didn't recognize. It's on the outskirts of town, and the only buildings nearby seem to be long-abandoned.

"Where are we?" I say, looking to Kaiden, and he looks simply defeated. He reaches out, squeezing my knee, turning reluctantly to face me.

"The end of the road, Princess," he says before the cop opens his door and yanks him out.

Everything is rusted, the building almost cavernous as obsolete equipment littered the corners. Windows are broken in and every high-heeled step echoed around us.

My legs barely work, and I have to be pushed along by the young officer, prodded to keep walking towards my doom.

I can't believe that this is how it all ends.

That we got away, tried to do the right thing, and that the end comes here, in a dirty, abandoned warehouse.

It's not where I thought I'd be at this point in my life. I'd wanted to go to college, better myself. Be someone Mom and Dad would be proud of.

Not someone dying with my step-brother at the hands of some drug dealer.

"I heard about last night," comes a voice echoing

through the building, though I didn't recognize it, and despite the sun outside, I can't see anyone. There are still so many shadows, hiding places, and the voice sounds like it's all around us.

Footsteps echo as the cops stand their guard on either side of Kaiden and me. Did Ryder pay them off? Did he have that much influence in this town?

Kaiden stays silent at my side, his hands wrapped into tight, angry fists. He took a hell of a beating, but he certainly looked ready for more.

"I'm disappointed," the voice continues, and I can pinpoint it to the left corner of the building, just hidden between a bunch of rebar. "I thought you weren't willing to go all the way."

The man who appears a second later isn't someone I know. He rivals Kaiden's six and a half foot tall stature, though he's not as muscular, just big. His suit is tailored and tattoos run down his hands and up his throat, making him look menacing. Like a thug gone professional.

"I didn't want to go all the way, but I didn't have an option," Kaiden spits back with a sneer. "And load of good that did me."

The man laughs, cruelly, and starts down the stairs towards us, his eyes on me.

"Ah, yes. Abigail. The one you were willing to throw away years of your life for. Good years, too," he adds on with a glance to Kaiden. "The little sister."

I hear a low, angry grunt from Kaiden as he tries

to move forward, but a firm hand on his shoulder stops him, the cop giving him a glare.

"Axel, I swear to God, if you hurt her, you're going to regret it," he says, and suddenly it all makes sense. Their boss. Ryder's boss.

Wait, they'd talked about taking out Ryder before?

I look at Kaiden with wide eyes, but Axel comes nearly a foot away from us, and he's not scared at all. Why should he be? There are two cops holding us hostage, just waiting for his word to...do what, exactly?

Kill us?

A shiver goes down my spine and I look at the boss. He's huge and intimidating, but Kaiden doesn't seem to back down.

"You two stink of sex," he says with disdain, and I get a pit in my stomach of nerves and fear, but he brushes the thought off without a second more.

"Well, Kaiden, I'm glad you decided to return to me, because now that I know you're man enough, we're going to have a conversation. And while we have a conversation, Abigail is going to be in my office, waiting for you to come to her rescue," he says, and instantly, the young officer behind me starts pushing me forward.

"No!" I cry out, reaching out for Kaiden as he lunges for me. Axel and the other officer, though, keep him pinned.

"Leave her alone!" Kaiden orders, his voice booming and angry, but Axel doesn't back down.

"Abby! It'll be fine, okay? You just wait for me, I'm going to come back for you," Kaiden promises as I'm dragged towards the stairs, the officer ignoring my struggles as he picks me up and throws me over his shoulder.

I reach out, trying to grab Kaiden, but I'm already way too far, tears streaming down my face.

"Kaiden!" I sob, kicking my legs. I can't be taken from him! Not after all we'd been through, not after all we've done! For years we've denied what we mean to one another, and I can't lose that now. I struggle and writhe, the guard tightening his hold on my naked thighs as he moves off the steps.

I grab onto the railing, and for a moment, I think he's going to fall, bringing me with him, and I can picture myself falling forward, hitting my head on the concrete, so I let go and he catches his balance once more.

"I'll be back, Princess! Don't doubt your Prince Charming," Kaiden orders. "I love you!"

"I love you too!" I cry out, my voice so hard and filled with terror, but there's no stopping what's happening. Seconds later I'm in a small, dingy office, and the cop is trying to handcuff me to the chair.

The door is shut, and I can't hear anything else. There's no sound except for the metal scraping the floor as I struggle to escape the cop's grasp.

He backhands me, and it carries more force than I thought someone like him could deliver, and I gasp.

In that second he manages to cuff me to the chair, rendering me immobile.

"Just fucking sit still if you know what's good for you," he warns as he grabs some of those plastic zip ties, bringing one to my bare ankle, binding me to the chair. Both my hands and legs are bound before I know it.

He looks me in the eyes as he brings a gag to my mouth, his lip twitching in a strange manner.

"Don't piss off Axel. Just sit and be good," he orders with a tone of warning that sends a shiver up my spine.

I nod, but my stomach is roiling.

What's happening down there? And where is Axel taking Kaiden?

KAIDEN

"You know what I can do to her," Axel says to me, and I have never wanted so bad to fucking kill someone as I do right now.

He has Abigail captive, and feeling powerless isn't something I like. I want to head butt these two assholes, run up the stairs and save her. Then just run away.

This is all my fault.

I should have never told her to come back here, but I had hoped that if we got rid of this bullshit looming over me, we could be free. I'm being naive, and that just makes me so much angrier.

"And you know what I can do for you," Axel says, not bothering to wait for my response. He knows me too well, anyways. That I'm a hothead but that I've never killed.

That I've never got myself in so over my head that I had to.

But he still asked me to kill Ryder, knowing I couldn't, and now this is his punishment for disobeying him.

He always has to up the ante.

"I'm not fucking killing anyone, Axel," I say, hoping my words sound terrifying despite the pain that's lacing them.

Abby wasn't wrong, I really do need to go to a hospital, but there's no time for those luxuries. At least the memory of her sucking me off can numb a bit of my agony.

"Yeah, well, kid? I think you will. Because if you don't, then I'm going to get to him, bring him back here, let him get his revenge on you via your little sister, and then I'll kill him myself. But you know I don't like killing people myself don't you?" he says coolly, and his words make me hate him more than anything else ever has.

Even Ryder doesn't piss me off this much.

"Ryder came here this morning, you know? Told me about the little stunt you pulled. And so now, you're going to finish the job, and then you're going to come back here, retrieve your little sister, and then..." he pauses, pacing in front of me, his arms folded.

He's not a muscular guy, but he's strong. I've seen him break people's fingers and hands just for pissing him off, but he always does it as a threat, not as an endgame. He leaves that to his lackeys. Like me.

Originally, the deal was that I could go free on the charges against me and take over Ryder's business, but I guess Axel's a smart enough guy to know that that isn't what I want anymore.

Still, his words surprise me.

"Once you finish up here, we're done. The DA will throw out the case, and you'll get the fuck out of here. Everyone wins," he says, offering his hands to heaven.

I sneer, the pain getting to me, so I just give a nod of my head.

"Let's get this done."

THE COP DRIVES me back to my place, and I grab a few things. Bullets, some cash left around, and a bit of clothing for Abby and myself. We're going to need it once we're out of here and trying to lay low.

I look in her drawers, the nightclub clothes she wears to work contrasting so much against the outfits she brought when she first moved in.

Prissy little blouses and skirts, all carefully pressed and folded, and I simply dump them in the backpack along with her laptop.

I sling it over my shoulder, look back at the world I'd made here, and walk away.

My bike's where I left it and I hop on.

Axel told me that Ryder was going to a doctor friend of his on the outskirts of town, and that he's going to be laying low there for a few days. He'll be alone for one hour, forty minutes from now, and I have to be there and take advantage of what might be my only opportunity to save Abigail and get us both out of this mess.

Usually riding my bike soothes me.

The wind whipping through my hair used to make me feel so free, but today it just feels like another burden. Another mask I have to wear to get what I want.

I drive the familiar roads, and I don't know how I'm going to do this. To actually pull the trigger? To see a man, living before me, and then take that from him?

Even though Ryder's an ass and deserves it, I just don't know that I can be the one to do it.

But I have to. That's what I have to do to save Abby, and that's what I'm going to do.

I stop outside the place, kicking down my stand and leaning my bike. I know he likely heard me coming up the gravel drive, but I still move slow and quiet, making sure that my steps don't make any more sound than they need to.

My gun's in my hands, cocked and ready, and I slow my breathing so that I can hear.

There's nothing, no sounds coming from out the

open windows, and I breathe a sigh of relief. Maybe he's asleep and up on pain meds. I did a number on his throat, and I can only imagine what a bitch that must be.

I go to the door and just as Axel promised, it's unlocked. Swinging it inwards I look around the aged kitchen, the table filled with drugs, and I have a bad feeling about this. If I'm caught here with a gun, that's going to be a lot more time than just three years.

This is fucking premeditated!

But I know better than to get stuck inside my head, and I shake off my fear and worries.

There's no use getting lost in my thoughts and fretting, that'll just get me killed.

I walk past the kitchen table, the smell of cat urine strong in the air as I move through to the living room. There's no one here, and I can hear the wheezing of someone just two doors down the hall.

This is it, I tell myself inwardly, psyching myself up.

I shake out my shoulders, loosening my arms as I make my way past the first bedroom. There's still the rhythmic wheezing, and I know that Ryder's in there, asleep.

Vulnerable.

The thought makes me sick to my stomach about what I've become but it doesn't matter. I keep going.

I nudge open the door, looking at him lying on

the bed and point my gun. His chest rises and falls as he struggles to breathe, the bandage around his throat soaked with blood.

Last night I stared down the gun, pointed at his head, and I pulled the trigger. I was so close to snuffing him out, but I couldn't. And now I hesitate.

And then I lower my gun.

I can't do it. There's gotta be another way to save Abby. I know the warehouse inside and out, and if she's locked in his office, all I'd have to do is scale the building and get out. I walk down the hall, back towards the kitchen, my mind reeling.

I place the gun down as I sit, trying to collect myself. *This is your only chance*, I chastise myself. *Be a man. Save your girl.*

But I look at the gun, and I know I can't. I stand up, moving for the door to leave when I realize I can't hear the wheezing anymore. I listen intently, straining my ears as I try to catch the familiar sound of safety, but there's nothing.

And then there's only blackness.

I don't know how long Kaiden's been gone and I've been left alone in this room. I'm chilly, my tank top and skirt doing nothing to keep out the chilliness of the warehouse and the cold metal chair pressing into me.

I'm still sweating, though, fear and anxiety making me unable to calm down or relax. I don't know what to do, because there's nothing I *can* do. Just sit and wait, bound to this chair. I don't even know if there's anyone else in the warehouse or if I'm all alone in here.

I haven't heard from anyone, and there's not even a clock to keep me company.

I find myself struggling. Not just with being bound in this chair, not just with being held captive by a drug gang, but even with who I am and who I want to be.

I see myself in college, studying and complaining to a friend about my grades or how hard a midterm was. That kind of thing is supposed to be the most dramatic thing happening to me in my life.

Instead, I'm in love with my step-brother, and I'm tied to a chair, not knowing when or if I'll ever see him again. Tears stream from my eyes, down over my cheeks only to drop onto my thighs, sending another shiver up my spine.

He has to come back.

He's my big brother, my hero.

He protected me from bullies and mean girl-friends. He'd always looked out for me, and then he just wasn't there anymore, but I understand so well why.

At least, now I do. Now I know what he was fighting so hard to resist doing.

But it can't be stripped from us! Not now! Not when we've finally come to terms, finally accepted those long-repressed desires!

I rock myself back and forth in my chair, trying to escape, to move closer to the door. I need to find out if there's anyone else out there. I can't hear anything from in here! The scraping is like nails on a chalkboard, but I ignore it as I shuffle closer and closer to the door. There's a window above it, and if I can tilt myself just so, maybe I can hear...

Though when I get nearer to the door, there's still nothing but the aching silence and loneliness. It has to have been hours since I was left here, the door locked behind the crooked cop. I still don't know how Axel managed to buy off the cops, but they were under his thumb as good as any. I'd thought of the town as the Wild West when I first moved here, but now I know that's truer than ever.

"Help!" I cry out through the gag, though I know it's fruitless. Even if someone could hear me, they weren't going to be my savior.

There's only one person with the power to get me out of here.

"Kaiden," I whimper, not for the first time. I remember back to my time in prison, to the realization that I really, truly love him. That I'd wanted him to rescue me from the trouble I'd gotten myself into, and how he showed up, proud and eager to help.

He didn't even hold it against me, bring it up as a jab. He just accepted it for what it was and let it go.

I rock the chair towards the door, trying to get it hooked under the door knob or break out the glass or something, but I can't do anything. I'm bound too tight, the handcuffs and zip ties digging into my skin and making it turn red the more I struggle. I'm absolutely helpless.

* * *

I AWAKE WITH A START, and I don't even remember falling asleep. My face is wet and feels gross, caked on tears tarnishing my skin. But then I hear the sound that must've woke me up in the first place. In the distance, a motorcycle is revving. It's coming from the opposite side of the building, and one of the broken out windows must be letting in that little bit of sound.

That siren call.

But I don't know it's Kaiden. He runs with a gang of people that all ride bikes, after all. For all I know, that could be Axel returned to punish me for Kaiden's failing to do whatever he wanted.

And what *did* he want? Was it for Kaiden to...?

I shake my head free of the thought. No, no, Kaiden couldn't do that. I know that he pulled the trigger last night, but it's not the same thing now.

He was trying to protect me.

Just like he's trying to do now.

I can't think like that! Kaiden isn't a killer, he'd find another way.

There's silence again, and I'm left alone to wonder if it was all a mirage, just me hearing things because of how scared I am. My ears strain once more, trying to detect anything from outside, or from in the rest of the warehouse, but there's nothing.

I start rocking my chair again, banging it against the door, trying to draw the attention of whomever it is. I know it's stupid, but I don't have any options!

I need to get out of here, and if only someone

could come in and talk to me, well, maybe there'd be a chance!

There's still no sounds, until suddenly I can feel the doorknob try to turn. My chair is lodged in under it, though, preventing it from opening, and I wonder if maybe I shouldn't keep it like that. Keep whoever is out there, coming for me, locked out.

Stay safe in here until I know for sure it's Kaiden.

And then I hear his voice.

"Abby, let me in," he says, and even though he's trying to project his voice loud enough for me to hear, it sounds so exhausted.

I shuffle away from the door, my chair tipping and nearly falling over in the process, but I manage to keep myself up straight.

He rushes in the second I'm free of the door and holds me close, his body pressed to mine awkwardly. He pulls out the wet gag from my mouth.

"The keys," I gasp, motioning to the desk in the corner of the room. "The cop, he put them in there."

Kaiden walks over to it with a limp, and when he turns back to me, I see that his shirt is bloody, a big gash up along his side. I wince in sympathetic pain as he disappears behind me, frantically undoing my handcuffs.

I rub my wrists, the raw flesh so bright red, hurting from being twisted and yanked in my useless attempts to break free. Next he grabs out his Swiss army knife, cutting the bindings on my ankles, and I leap up, wrapping my arms around him.

Tears stream down my face as he peppers my mouth with kisses, holding me tight despite all his bruises and the blood. I'm covered in it as well now, but I don't care.

I'm just so happy to have him back again.

"Come on," he says, guiding me to the door, letting me rest on him.

My body feels all out of sorts, exhausted and sore, and although I know he wants to lift me up and relieve me of the burden of walking, he's too hurt to help more than what he is already.

We make our way to the exit of the building, and there's no one else around. The cop cars are gone, as is Axel's bike, and me and Kaiden are left alone.

Free.

My arms wrap around him, the vibration of the bike going through me. I'm so exhausted, but the fact that I have Kaiden back is giving me a second wind.

So when he pulls over at a rest stop and suggests we take a few minutes to clean ourselves up in the bathroom, I know what he means.

I've never been put in so many life-or-death scenarios as I have recently, and it seems almost sick that it makes me want to appreciate life all the more. To clutch onto that bit of happiness I found with Kaiden, and never let it go.

Now that we're finally, blissfully alone, our passion can't be stopped. We need one another like we need air. After getting the keys from the gas station attendant, we both disappear into the cramped and dirty restroom.

I don't even mind as he lifts me up, resting me on top of the sink, spreading my legs as he goes to work at his belt. Quickly that's taken off, and he's pushing my panties to the side and sinking into me. It's only been a few hours since we were last together, and we don't have the luxury of romance.

We're both pressing into one another, unable to contain our need to just appreciate the fact that we're both still alive. That we made it out in one piece, and now, we're free.

His bare cock strikes into my depths as his mouth moves along my throat.

I feel filthy and wrong, my hands clasping the sink as I grind my hips into his, but it feels so right at the same time.

I scream, no longer caring who hears, and he pounds me harder. The tapping digs into my back, and the sink threatens to break under the weight and force of his thrusts.

One of my hands reaches up, wrapping around his neck, nails digging into him as he sucks my skin so hard I know it'll leave a mark. And I want it. I want him to mark me, to claim me as his, body, heart, and soul.

I scream again as he ruts into me, his teeth biting at my skin, my head spinning with desire and need. I can't believe how good it feels being fucked like this, to be handled so roughly, but it's like a celebration of life.

Of just being able to experience such pleasure and pain together in one.

The mirror behind me stabs into my back, tearing my shirt even more, but I don't care. It all just serves as a glorious reminder that we're alive, that we made it, and I wrap my legs and arms around him. He lifts me from the sink, instead smacking my back against the wall as he holds me tight, rutting into me so hard.

His lips are bruising and painful on mine, his every action filled with passion and joy, without consideration for being delicate. And I don't want him to be soft. I don't want him to treat me like a doll.

I need to feel this, to feel him in his unhinged state and truly appreciate what his amazing body can do.

We're a mess of dirt and unwashed hair, the smell of sex rising up off of us as I scream and cry, not caring who can hear.

I want everyone to hear.

I want the whole world to know what a sex god Kaiden is, and that he's all mine.

His hand goes to my jaw, his fingers hard as he explores my neck, my skin, my ear.

His hands knit into my hair, and he brings my mouth back to his, his teeth biting my lower lip, making me bleed, and I can only moan into it. He tastes like my blood, and I press my tongue to his, the muscle vibrating with my constant sounds of pleasure as he takes me hard in the dirty washroom.

I don't know how long we go at it, how many times he whips me around, slamming me from one wall to another. I'm filthy, and dirty, and his as he presses me to the floor, staring down at me as he grabs my thighs and makes my ankles wrap around his throat.

He's never been so deep, never been so hard with me, but I've never been so wet, and that lets him slap in easily.

I feel like he's bruising me all over, my ass, my shoulders, my head, my mouth, and I'm shocked at how much I love it.

How much I crave more.

"Kaiden!" I scream, not caring that there's someone at the door, knocking, telling us to get out right now. I don't care, I want them to hear! To know that I'm being fucked in a slummy restroom by my hot step-brother.

"Kaiden, fuck!" I cry out, and he growls, his hands on my hips, holding me in place. My thighs and legs ache as he stretches them back, forcing me to take him deeper and deeper into my body, his pace all the while growing faster and faster.

I can't believe how much it hurts, how good it feels, and he grabs my breast through my flimsy top.

There's no more delicate pinches, no teasing to

his actions. He's serious, his hand gripping my small breast so hard that I know I'm going to have a bruise there, and I scream.

His other hand goes to my clit, not rubbing, just pressing down on it, making those sparks appear before my eyes.

He's like a whole different person. Not the man I knew who took home those random floozies and gave them a good time, not the sweet man who dirty talked me into bed and made me want him.

This Kaiden is an *animal*, unhinged and raw, and he's simply taking what he needs from my body, what he wants. What I need, what I want. I cry out as the tops of my thighs press against my stomach, trapping his hand in place, and when I open my eyes I see him staring at me with such intensity.

His green eyes move over my face, over my body, down to where his cock is firmly rooted in my pussy and the way my pale skin parts for his ruddy tool. It's so obscene, and so hot, and the man knocking at the door can't stop that, not even as we can hear the keys begin to work in the door. They must have finally got the spare set.

"Hurry!" I beg him, needing my relief, needing to finish this, whatever it is. Whatever primal need that's driving us both on. I fear that if we're interrupted, we'll never recover.

We'll never find our way back.

And he presses my legs back even further as he begins to rub my clit harder and with more ferocity. His rough hand is usually so skilled and careful, but this time, it's brute force to match the rest of him, and I love it.

It sends a jolt down my spine and then the waves of pleasure descend.

I scream as the door clicks above me, opening and knocking me in the head.

"Sir!" The man yelps, looking at the scene of the two of us on the floor, slaves to passion and one another's bodies.

There's no stopping Kaiden, though, not then. He's a wild beast, and his hips keep moving as my pussy squeezes his tool, begging him to come. Begging for him to meet that peak with me.

"Kaiden!" I scream again, and another tremble goes through me, my muscles tightening and massaging his cock, and I can feel it start to swell, warning me of what's to come.

He thrusts in harder as the man grabs at his shirt, trying to tear him away from me, but there's no stopping him.

"Abby!" he growls as he hits his peak, his pleasure flushing his face, his entire body tightening before he stabs himself deep inside me, spilling that seed against my womb once more, flooding my pussy with his hot come.

My legs are still pinned between my shoulder

and his, and he doesn't stop, not fully, not even after he reaches his peak. He gives a few more thrusts, making sure that every last drop of his come is lodged within me before he finally glares up at the gas station attendant.

"I'm done," he says, swatting off the other man's hand as if it were a disgusting gnat he didn't want touching him.

"You mind giving us a second?" he asks, though it's not a question. He grinds his cock into me, the flared tip pressed against my deepest recesses, as if in an example to the attendant who stares a little too long.

I don't know what we must look like, filthy and dirty, rolling around and fucking on the floor of a gas station, but a huge part of me doesn't care.

I have Kaiden back, and that's all that matters.

The attendant finally leaves, giving us a few moments of privacy, though I know he's waiting just outside the door to, what? Chastise us?

The thought makes me laugh out loud as Kaiden pulls from me, and he gives me an odd look. I shake my head, and bite down on my lip for a moment.

"I think this is the first time anyone's ever caught us being bad together," I giggle, and Kaiden begins to laugh as well.

"Yea, you were always so good at not being caught, Princess," he says, trying to keep his tone light as he turns on the tap, washing himself off.

"And this time here you are, screaming like a banshee."

I titter nervously as I quickly wash myself as well, and we make our way past the judgmental stare of the gas station employee, both of us laughing like kids.

$\mathcal{I}$ have a little bounce to my step, and I know I should be embarrassed at being caught having sex in a public bathroom, or at least feel like I need a shower— which I do—but I just feel so *great*. All of that aggression and worry and lust all built up and just had to erupt.

And *holy wow* did it erupt.

I look up at him, smiling and expecting to see the same look on his face, but he looks... different some-how. Maybe it's just the pain of his wounds, and I know we need to get to a pharmacy at the very least, but it's not the same. Not even the same as last night, when he was in plenty of pain.

I slow down, standing near his bike, and tug his hand.

"What's wrong?" I ask, glancing back at the

building and checking that no one had been following us.

He shakes his head, patting my shoulder gently.

"It's nothing. I just need to get to the store and get some bandages," he replies, but I know there's more to it. He's holding something back, but he gives me a look that warns me to drop it.

We climb back on his bike, but suddenly it doesn't feel the same. It doesn't feel as comfortable, as safe. I'm not sure what just happened between the time that we were rutting on the bathroom floor like animals and now, but there's definitely something off.

I wrap my arms loosely around his waist as he starts us off. I'm not sure where he's taking us, but I'm too exhausted to protest. The sun is starting to set off in the distance, a few clouds dulling the light and making it seem almost ominous.

We can't really talk with the roar of the motor-cycle between us, so I rest my head against his spine, listening to the rapid beating of his heart.

What did he have to do to rescue me? What is it that's bothering him?

My heart begins to beat faster, matching the pace of his, and I go over the options in my head. That he escaped, that he came back and rescued me, without anyone getting in his way. But I know that's not what happened.

The huge gash along his stomach didn't come from nothing, barely bandaged with an old t-shirt.

But I'm too scared to think of the other options.

Did he hurt someone?

Or worse?

The thought makes my blood go cold.

How could I have someone's murder on my hands? How can I live with myself knowing someone else died for me?

I shake the thought out of my mind. I know Kaiden. I know he wouldn't do that, wouldn't kill someone in cold blood. He beat up bullies, he was always in a fight, but he'd never kill someone, I'm sure of that.

But the way he's grown so cold since our quickie...

It's an hour later, and we're in another town about a hundred miles away from where Kaiden lives and about fifty miles from where we grew up.

I vaguely remember driving through on my way in, and Kaiden pulls up next to a bank that looks to be closed. He turns off the ignition, then reaches into his pocket, handing me a small key.

"This is the place the money is, Princess. Come here tomorrow, show them the key, and tell them you have a safety deposit box you need to open. Six, five, three, one. You got that, Princess?"

I nod, my eyes moving over his. There's no spark there, no fire, just... shadows.

"Six, five, three, one," I repeat back to him, and he nods, leaning in and kissing my forehead.

He turns on the motorcycle once more, and a few moments later, we're pulled up next to a pharmacy where I see a strange sight.

My car. Sitting in the parking lot, abandoned and in the dark. How did he get that here from Axel's place?

I furrow my brow, not quite sure what to make of it as Kaiden dismounts.

"I have to get some stuff for my wounds, Princess, but..."

I stare at him, dread hanging heavy in my heart.

"Don't," I say, my voice sounding so soft and scared. The parking lot is dimly lit, and I can see the pain in his expression as he shakes his head.

"Princess, this is it... I can't be the man you deserve," he says, and the words cut through me like a knife.

It's like he just ripped out my heart and threw it on the ground, and I clutch my chest. I'm not able to breath, my throat constricted, and he reaches out instinctively to lay a hand on my arm, helping me stand straight.

Tears blur my vision as he stares down at me.

"I can't change what I did, Abby. What I had to do to get you back."

"Stop," I plead with him. I don't want him to say anymore.

This is supposed to be our happy ending. This is supposed to be our happily ever after.

He presses his lips to my forehead, brushing some of my hair from it so tenderly. He inhales, and I tremble against him, trying not to cry. Not to let him see me lose myself.

But this can't be the end!

"He's dead, Abby. I killed him, so that you can live. But that wasn't your choice," he says as if he instinctively knows I'd blame myself. Maybe he does.

"I didn't want to, but I had to, but no matter what Axel says, I'll never be free of my past. Not totally. But you can be," he says, his index finger curling under my jaw, making me look up at him.

"I don't care!" I cry out, thrusting myself into him and making him cringe in agony. "I don't care, I just want you!"

But he kisses me again and shakes his head, and my whole world comes crashing down upon me. He's resolute, and I hate him so much at this moment.

He's supposed to protect me, to be the one that will always be here for me, and now he's leaving me again?

"Princess, I need you gone by the time I come back out. They're going to be watching me," he says before he presses his lips to mine, quieting another sob from escaping.

How am I supposed to just leave? To let him walk away from what we have?

My chest heaves, and my knees feel like they're going to buckle and let me fall, but Kaiden lets me go, and somehow I manage to stay on my feet. He grabs the backpack that was stuffed in the saddle, handing it to me.

"I got your laptop and some of your clothes and things. It's not much, but it's not safe to go back there, ever. Do you understand? You have to stay as far from that place as you can, and once you get that money from the bank tomorrow, never come back here either. Start fresh, somewhere where they can never find you again."

I can barely make sense of his words even, but I'm too exhausted to fight him anymore. He's made up his mind.

He's decided for the both of us what I'm to do.

He kisses my forehead again.

"Go to college, Abby. Make a life for yourself. Make me proud, okay? You always said I was your hero, but you've always been mine, Princess. Please... Please don't make this harder than it needs to be."

I don't. I can't. I'm too dazed, too sad and disappointed and deflated to do anything more than drag myself to my car, chucking my bag in the passenger seat and slumping down.

If he doesn't want me here, then there's no reason for me to stay.

As he makes his way into the pharmacy, his shoulders are slumped, and I watch my step-brother turn his back and leave me once more.

All I can do is cry. Big, ugly tears, my skin still holding the imprints and sensations of where and how he touched me. The things he did to me. The things I wanted him to do to me.

And now it's all over.

FIVE DAYS LATER

ive days. It's been five days since I last saw Kaiden, since he walked out of my life. I'm now richer than I could have ever hoped, but it's all hollow, because there's nothing I want.

I've had to drive around listlessly for a long time, not sure what to do or where to go. I've had to avoid everything and everyone I ever knew, and I don't have anyone left.

No family, no friends, no Kaiden.

The money sits in my glove box and beneath the seats, taunting me, teasing me about all the things I can't use it for, but it doesn't matter. The fog of depression weighs heavy on my shoulders, and I just don't care about anything anymore.

On the fourth day, I found myself driving through the same town I'd been arrested in, and thought back to Sarah. About the fact that she'd three times been arrested for prostitution, and I knew they wouldn't come down easy on her.

So I set up an anonymous way of paying a lawyer that came highly recommended on *backpage* by other escorts, and asked him to help her out. I figured if there's anything that the money could do, helping a person in need might at least make me feel a bit better, but it didn't.

Instead, I feel just as hollow as I did before.

I make my way north, past all the familiar landmarks, all the memories of family vacations, and all my time with Kaiden. He was like a rollercoaster, bringing me to such highs and lows, but after the ride is over, you're always disappointed by how short the whole thing was.

He's always going to abandon me. I know that now. That when things get rough, he's going to run, and he's always going to do it his own way.

I don't know how I feel about that, but it gives me a small bit of comfort to know that this is just how it will be and that it's nothing I did wrong.

I'm just destined to be alone.

The highway stretches out before me, and for hours, I keep going through the vast nothingness until a sign catches my attention. San Francisco is up ahead, not one hundred miles away. I've never been there, not even for a visit. My parents always hated the big cities and preferred camping to driving on the busy streets.

Maybe this is my chance to make something of myself. To do something new and exciting.

Even that thought can't relieve the ache in my heart.

"Are you sure?"

"Yea, I'm sure, Becky!" I say, my voice shriller than I intend. There's no way this can be right. I can't be pregnant. Not now. Not when I'm on my own and just starting school.

It's two months after Kaiden abandoned me at the pharmacy, and I haven't had my period since then, but that doesn't matter.

This just... it can't be happening to me. No.

Fear and anguish rush through me, but there's something more, too. Excitement. I don't even want to think about it, and I try to push it down, snuff it out, but I can't deny that it's there, burning within me.

An excuse to reach out to him!

"Oh my God, Gail! You're pregnant!" She says it with enthusiasm but tones it down to gauge my reaction, but even so, she could have no idea why I look and feel so distraught. I never told anyone at the University of San Francisco about Kaiden, or even that I have a step-brother. Not that many people care.

Becky's pretty much my only real friend, but she's been a lot of fun and really important to getting me out of my slump.

She's toured me around the city, taken me to some of the best restaurants, but it's always been a bit disappointing. It's always been missing Kaiden.

I haven't heard from him since, and I've avoided looking.

If he didn't want me in his life, then that's his choice.

"So who's the father?" she asks, her tone sly, like I've been hiding something. "It's not Jack, is it? That guy is-"

"It's not Jack."

"Oh thank God!" she says, rolling her eyes heavenward. "The way he looks at you, you know, I was starting to wonder."

"Ew, Becky. No, it's not him. You don't know the guy," I say, and I wonder, for a second, if I knew him either.

"So what are you going to do?"

"I'm... I'm not sure. Maybe just raise it by myself."

"What? Don't be ridiculous, you're not even going to tell him?"

I shake my head and she looks mortified.

"If I got pregnant, I'd be sure as hell telling the guy and getting some child support at least. I mean, raising a baby isn't cheap, Gail," she says, her voice holding so much concern. "I mean, especially when you're only nineteen. Maybe you should think adoption..."

She looks at me with those big, green eyes of hers, and they remind me of Kaiden's. I wonder how he'd react.

If he'd be excited, or if it'd just be another bother.

He already gave me more than enough to cover child support.

But I can't deny the fact that I want him to know. He deserves to, after all we've been through.

I nod my head, brushing some of my dyed brown hair behind my ear. I'd taken Kaiden seriously about starting new.

When I moved, I started going by Gail, dyed my hair, changed my wardrobe, everything. I even started going to school, dreaming of the day that maybe I could be a lawyer. Start working to really help people in need, find some purpose to my life.

Becky leans in, touching my face gently.

"It'll be okay, I promise. But you should really tell him at least. C'mon, if you liked him enough to sleep with him, how bad can he be?"

It doesn't take me long to track down Kaiden.

I took him seriously when he said to start fresh, but apparently he didn't take his own advice. He had apparently put a down payment on mom and dad's old house.

It was kind of bitter-sweet to think of him back in the home we grew up in. We shared so much in those walls.

The drive back was harder than I expected. Once I started passing familiar buildings and homes once more, each brought a rush of memories with it, coming on faster and faster as I drove into town.

It's middle of the day on Saturday, a month after I found out I was pregnant. I tracked him down within a day, but I just can't bring myself to do it.

Not until I know for sure that nothing is going to happen with the baby.

I'm terrified, though, still.

I have no idea what he'll say, what seeing me will bring up in him.

What I'll feel at seeing him again.

It's only been three months since we parted ways. It feels like an eternity, yet at the same time, it feels like no time at all has passed, and I drive a bit slower out of fear more than anything.

I've brushed my hair, letting the dark locks spill around my neck, a casual shirt and jeans hiding most of my body.

I'd gotten so comfortable wearing revealing clothes around the bar, but now that I'm enrolled in college, I've gotten back to my more conservative outfits. It just feels more appropriate, anyways.

To be a bit hidden from him. To protect myself—and him—from our lusts. From our history.

I didn't tell him I was coming, though, and that makes me nervous. I don't want him to know. I just wanted to put off talking to him as long as possible.

But when I pull up in the driveway of our old home, and I see his bike, I can barely bring myself to get out of the vehicle.

When he comes to the window, though, and I see the light and excitement on his face, it pulls at me.

Draws me in, like it was his siren song, and I'm his willing victim.

He opens the door for me, pulling me out and hugging me tight, just like nothing ever happened.

And once more, I fall under his spell and remember why I've loved him so much all these years. I pull away, trying not to lose myself to his rugged charm, but I'm hopeless. He's covered up a bit, a shirt covering the myriad of tattoos and, I'd guess, more than a few scars.

I look down at the ground, suddenly struck mute and shy.

"Abby, God, why didn't you call? I could've..." he trailed off. He knew there was nothing he could've done, and for a second, I wonder if he's forgotten how he left me. That he abandoned me.

And then it strikes him, wiping the smile from his face, and he steps aside, letting me in, suddenly more formal.

"You want some tea?"

"Sure."

I go into the old hallway, following the familiar path to the kitchen. He looks so good, though there's a bit of a limp to his step, and I guess it's from the fight. He didn't get medical attention for a while, maybe that caused some damage.

He puts on the kettle, and I look around at the sparsely decorated room. He doesn't have much, but it seems like he was able to salvage some stuff from mom and dad, and memories wash over me.

"How've you been? Your hair is great."

He shakes me out of my reverie, and I give him a smile and a nod.

"Thank you. And I'm good, fine. I enrolled in college, started last month," I say, licking my lips.

I went over it in my mind a thousand times how I'd tell him, but every time it fell flat. And I know, at least in part, it's because I don't know whether to be happy or not about the news.

He leans against the counter, his biceps bulging and looking so good. I remember how they felt wrapped around me for those whirlwind hours we were finally, blissfully together, and it brings a flush to my cheeks and a heat to my loins.

I'm actually upset by the fact that I still want him —annoyed, even. By the fact that when he talks, I'm still looking at that tongue stud, remembering how it felt against my pussy.

And now I'm paying the price.

I sit at the table, my purse resting at my feet, as I look up at him. Instantly I regret it, as I feel even smaller now, but I don't want to stand and draw attention to my discomfort.

"What about you?" I ask, looking around. "Guess you got the bail money returned?"

He nods, a sheepish smile on his lips.

"Yep. Just enough to get this place out of foreclosure and a few things from the auction. It's not much, but it's a start."

I wonder if he regrets giving me the money, but I

know that's not true. He seems perfectly content without me in his life, and without the money in his life.

I swallow, nodding.

"That's good. It's nice to have it in good hands," I say, but my voice cracks, and he instantly comes over to me, his face marred with concern.

"Abby, what's wrong?"

I shake my head, wiping away a stray tear.

"It's nothing, nothing," I swear, but the words sound hollow and I know it.

His finger hooks in underneath my chin, making me look at him, stare into those beautiful green eyes. I long for him, even still, even after all he's done, but I can't let myself fall for him again. I can't let myself be hurt.

It's not just me anymore, but for the baby, too.

I have to protect us both from the stress and the agony of Kaiden's fickleness, and thinking he knows best.

I chew on my lower lip, nerves coiling within my gut, making me regret ever coming here.

I wish I'd just called him or sent a message online, but I wanted to do the right thing. But doing the right thing feels so terrible, like my stitches have been torn open.

"I have something I need to tell you," I say, my voice soft, and the kettle interrupts me with its whistle.

He cringes and takes it off the stove, coming back to me without pouring up my tea, though this time he doesn't touch my chin, doesn't touch me at all, and my heart turns to ice.

"Is it the money?" he asks, his voice filled with worry. "Did something happen to it?"

I shake my head.

"Axel?"

I shake my head again, and he opens his mouth to ask something else and I silence him with my words.

"I'm pregnant."

Two simple, easy words, said billions of times over the course of humanity. So why did they feel so wrong?

He takes a step back, as if I'd just turned poisonous, and I stand up, quickly.

"This was a bad idea," I say, grabbing my purse, but he reaches out and holds my wrist firm.

"You're pregnant?" he asks, his voice dark, as if he hadn't heard me right the first time, and I nod.

"But... who?"

Anger floods through me, and I spin to face him, fire in my eyes.

"Who?" I ask, my voice rising. "What the fuck, Kaiden? Who? What do you think I am, huh? Just some floozy slut like all the rest of the girls you bring home?"

I've held onto so much anger, anger at him controlling so much of my life, anger at him making all the decisions that affect both of us, and I can hardly contain it.

"I thought you were on the pill!" he argues as he takes a step back, looking shocked at my outburst, but I don't feel anywhere near to done.

"On the *pill*? I was a virgin, Kaiden, and intended on keeping it that way!"

He takes another step back, leaning against the counter like I just punched him in the gut, and I feel a moment of satisfaction. I throw my purse over my shoulder and start towards the door, but he's faster than me, and he grabs both of my shoulders, pulling me to face him.

"So what now?" he asks, his voice softer, more filled with care and concern, but it's too little, too late.

"So now you know," I reply, trying to make my voice cold, but it comes out with a tremble of pain that I know he can sense.

He pushes me to the wall, stopping me from leaving, and I stare up at him aghast.

"Let me go."

"I can't," he protests, and his mouth moves to silence my words, his pierced tongue running against my upper lip as he presses his body to mine. He's already stiff against my stomach, grinding there, and for a moment I'm rendered dumb.

He tastes so good, and I kiss him back, the

passion between us mounting. I want him so bad, now more than ever, and I moan into his mouth.

"I want you," he whispers between kisses, his mouth trailing down my neck, over my collarbone, down along the fabric of my top as he pulls up the bottom of it. He exposes my stomach, still smooth but with a slight bump, to his mouth, and I want more than anything to lose myself in him again.

But I can't.

I push him away, his back hitting against the other side of the hallway, and I run out the door.

I sit on my bed, my headphones on. I just need to blare out all the badness, all the sorrow and loss.

Four months, and the morning sickness hasn't totally gone away, though I think at least part of it is due to missing him.

Wanting him back in my life.

I haven't heard from Kaiden since that horrible day, but the memory of his hands and mouth on me once more ignited that passion I'd quelled with the anger and rage of being abandoned.

But he didn't mean it.

If he did, I would've heard from him by now.

I flip through the adoption pamphlet Becky gave me, but I don't feel right about it. I don't feel right about any of it. I should've been more careful, more cautious, but he had me wrapped around his finger.

And now I'm paying the price.

Tossing the pamphlet aside, I sigh and pick up my phone. Even my old favorite songs aren't perking me up. Maybe I should try to find something more upbeat.

But when I turn on the screen, there's a text from a number I don't recognize. Probably another stupid reminder about some clothing sale I accidentally signed up for.

But when I swipe down, my heart stops.

Princess, I know I don't deserve you, but I want to. More than anything. Can we talk?

Tears spring to my eyes, and I don't know if it's the hormones or not, but I swipe them away quickly. My lower lip trembles, and the rest of the world is forgotten.

I stare for so long at that message, reading it over and over again. My heart starts racing, my palms going sweaty as I wonder what to say.

He's just going to blow you off, I chide myself, but I don't want to believe it. Not this time. Not now.

If ever I'm going to give him the benefit of the doubt, it has to be now.

Talk about what? I reply, and the second I hit send, I start wondering if it's too terse.

If he's going to think I'm still mad.

You are still mad, my subconscious reminds me, but that doesn't stop me from staring at my phone.

Every time the screen goes black again, I swipe it back on, the anticipation killing me.

Luckily, he doesn't keep me waiting for long.

I want to make it up to you. Can we meet? You know our spot on Big Bear Lake?

Big Bear Lake?

That was where...

I shake my head free of the memory of his mouth lingering so near to mine, and swallow. My mouth feels dry, my breathing increased. Big Bear Lake is still a seven-hour drive if traffic is good.

Do I really want to put myself in that position?

But even as I antagonize over it, I'm texting him back.

When?

This weekend?

And nothing within me can stop me from sending back:

OK.

I put the phone down, staring up at the ceiling.

What am I doing? Why does my heart keep tugging me towards pain?

But for the first time in so long, I find a restful sleep, a smile upon my lips and the image of Kaiden in the front of my mind.

ABIGAIL

The drive is long, giving me ample time to fret about what I'm doing. What choices I'm making.

I could've just flown, but I was afraid that I'd get there and be stuck with no way out, and I wanted options. That was worth the extra time.

Plus, it gave me an opportunity to mull over in my head precisely what I'm going to say to him. Or, more accurately, what he's planning on saying to me.

He wouldn't invite you all the way out here if it wasn't for a good reason, I remind myself, and I know it's true.

For all the things I could say about Kaiden, he wouldn't waste my time and my energy like this unless it was important. He has something planned, I just don't know what.

He made it pretty clear that being with him is *too dangerous* for me to handle, and now that I have a baby on the way?

Do I really want to get involved with the life he leads?

But then, he did go back to the old home, away from all of his 'friends' and associates, and he gave away his nest egg. But wouldn't that just make him want to break the law more?

I didn't bother asking what job he was working at when I came to see him because I was afraid of the answer.

Is that the life you want, Abigail? I ask myself, and I don't honestly know the answer to that. I'm getting close to the lake, and the beauty of the location manages to quiet my thoughts for a few blissful moments. There's a certain serenity to it, a peacefulness, and excitement and fear can't completely quash that.

We never had a cabin up here, we weren't as lucky as that, but there was a rental that our parents' friends had once in a while at the east end of the lake, and I drove the mildly familiar roads towards it.

I had dressed in a simple pair of pants and a sweater, knowing the lake would be cool this time of year, but I have the window down, the breeze blowing in my face. I never managed to get used to the brown hair and went back to blonde once more a few days after I saw Kaiden.

Maybe he just reminded me of who I was, and I like that girl. I don't want to be someone else.

And for all he's done... I don't want him to be someone else either.

But when I pull up in the driveway, and see him standing there in a fitted suit, my mouth hangs open in shock.

He still has the tattoos, still has the piercings and that deadly seductive glint in his eyes, but he's cleaned up, his hair slicked back, and my panties instantly grow wetter.

"Fucking Kaiden," I mutter to myself under my breath as he comes to the door, opening it for me and offering me his hand.

"Princess," he greets me, his dark voice so rich and alluring, "your Prince Charming has been waiting."

I have to bite down on my lower lip to keep it from trembling, blinking more rapidly to keep the tears from building in the corner of my eyes. The sun is beginning to set, the clouds in the sky turning beautiful pink and purples, only highlighting how much like a fairy tale this feels like.

He wraps his fingers within mine, guiding me towards the boat that waited for us at the docks. It isn't the same one that we'd been in all those years ago, but it's close. Small and intimate.

He hands me a life jacket, and I laugh, but the look he gives me says not to protest, and I put it on, watching him do the same. It's funny to me to see him being so cautious, especially after all we've been through.

He helps me into the boat, following after me, our knees brushing against one another's as he begins to row us out. He's been silent, and I don't know what to say. I'm a bit apprehensive about being away from dry land, but the water is a brilliant purple, the color of the sky reflected back at us, trees all around and giving us some privacy.

It's not until we're a good ways from shore that he puts aside the oars and looks at me earnestly.

"I owe you an explanation."

"You do," I say, though I'm having a harder time being upset with him.

His being my Prince Charming, my hero... it brings back so many powerful memories, so many memories I'd tried to bury over the years.

"I thought I was protecting you. That's why I ran. This time, the last time... I didn't want to corrupt you, drag you down with me, Abby. Look at me. I'm a mess without you," he says, nervously running his hand through his hair. It's endearing to see him so addled, though I try not to show it.

Instead, I just stare, waiting for him to continue.

"When I left, you were still just a kid. It would've

been wrong to stay, to believe that there could've been something between us."

"I was fifteen, Kaiden," I say with a roll of my eyes, "and you were only eighteen. We were both just kids."

"Yea, well, most people aren't going to look at it that way. Especially since... us... we were never supposed to be. Can you imagine what our parents would have said?"

"I try not to," I admit.

"Exactly! And the people of the town? They'd look at me like I was some... predator. So I left, I did the right thing, Abby. I wanted to give you a chance, to be your own person. To find a guy your own age and..."

"And what?"

"I don't know, get together, fall in love. The things you're supposed to do."

Tears flood my eyes, and I don't know if I'm angry, hurt, or just sad.

"I was already in love."

"A crush," he says, brushing it off. "That's... that's all I thought it was, and if I was gone, then you could move on."

My lower lip trembles, but he doesn't stop.

"But I couldn't get you off my mind, and I got fired from my first job. That's when Ryder found me. I was desperate not to come back, not to ruin your life, and he took advantage of that. Groomed me to be his right-hand man, taught me everything he knew. I was only working with him a year when he took me out into the desert and made me watch him shoot his last second, Abby. After that, I knew I couldn't come back and lead him to you."

That was why he stopped visiting?

He reaches out, touching my knee, and I suck in a breath.

"So I did what I had to. I survived, and I tried to find pleasure where I could, but you don't know how bad I wanted to just come home. I told them... I told them my family was all dead. I don't know if they believed me, but that's why I didn't stay after the funeral. It... it was why I didn't want you to live with me, but I just couldn't stand the thought of you being homeless and without anything," he says, his voice breaking.

"I agreed to take the fall for him because I thought it would be easier for all of us. Easier for me. I was selfish. I thought it would make it easier not to see you, but it didn't. Abby, every day since I left home," he says, leaning in, his hand touching my face and wiping away a tear I didn't know had fallen, "all I could think about was you. The way you make me feel."

My lip trembles, and his thumb traces along it.

"Axel told me I had to kill Ryder in order to rescue you, to get out of these charges. That was the deal, but when I got to the house, I couldn't do it. I was trying to figure something else out when Ryder came up behind me. He knocked me out, and the only reason he didn't shoot me was because he said I wasn't worthy of a quick death. That I wasn't half the man his old partner was."

Kaiden's breathing grows heavier, his voice turning husky.

"He tied me up, started cutting me. Said he was going to pull my guts out all slow like, but he must've still been on some powerful sedatives, because his knots were sloppy and I was able to get out and kill him before he got that far."

He licks his lips, his tongue ring glinting and teasing me for a second.

"Axel said he'd let you and me go, scot-free, but Abby, these aren't the people that let things go. This will always be over my head. Always."

I look at him, tears blurring my vision.

"I don't care," I whimper, and he leans in, his hand still caressing my face tenderly. "I don't care about any of that, I just want you! I've always wanted you!"

He shakes his head, and he sounds so sad.

"Abby, I'm not the man you deserve. I can never be your hero, not after what I've done. Not after the things I've had to do."

But I lean in, and I do the thing that I should've done all those years ago.

I kiss him.

Salty tears are shared between us, but I don't care. I can't resist him anymore, I can't deny my feelings and what I want. I tried, and he tried, and we both ended up miserable and shattered fragments of ourselves.

He holds me to him, his hand lacing into my hair as he kisses me with such urgency and passion.

"I should have kissed you that day," he murmurs as we pull apart, his green eyes locked on mine. "I should've just given in. We're no good apart, Princess. Well, I mean, you've done great, but I'm not great apart from you," he says, and I can't help but let out a laugh.

The sun has disappeared, leaving behind a surreal glint to the world as the stars begin to flicker into the night sky, the moon burning bright.

"I can't... I can't handle this alone, Abby. I can't be the man I want to be without you by my side," he says, and he shifts, reaching for something behind him that I hadn't noticed before. It's a small little velvet bag, and he hands it to me.

"Abigail, I know people won't understand us. I know people won't get why we were or how, and they might think we're... sick freaks for what we feel. But I know you don't care, and I don't care. I can't keep you safe if I don't know where you are, and I... There's no light or joy in my life without you, Princess."

I open the little bag and gasp.

A ring?

I pull it out, staring at him with my mouth dropped open. The diamond is round and huge, a classic shape.

"This... is my mom's first wedding ring," he admits, licking his beautiful lips nervously. "She put it in storage once she married your dad, but she could never give it away. For all my mom and your dad had, he was her first love, and it meant a lot to her. I think it's only suiting that I give it to you," he says before shifting.

The boat rocks, and his hands go to either side of my hips, holding me steady as he gets down on one knee.

"Abigail... will you-"

"Yes!" I cry out, wrapping my arms around him, the sudden shift nearly toppling the boat over, and he hugs me tight to his broad chest. I put the ring on my finger, and it glints in the dusky light, looking so elegant and refined.

And then his mouth is on mine, covering me with kisses, his tongue lashing against me, and we're both instantly slaves to the thing we'd denied and run from for so long.

The rocking of the boat inhibits us, but only at first. It wasn't long before Kaiden's big, strong limbs have us steadied.

We were lost in each other's lips, kissing and lashing our tongues against one another as he took hold of my hips, squeezing my sides. Those strong, hard hands such a long missed feeling. So familiar even after so long.

The lash of his studded tongue such a titillating thrill.

It's all coming back so fast, so natural. Even though ours was a lust given bloom for only a short while.

It isn't easy. Our lust is tempered by physics, by our life jackets, by the fact that I just *had* to wear pants to our meeting. Maybe I thought it would serve as protection against my desires, but instead, it's just another hindrance that keeps me from feeling his body against mine right now.

I wrap my arms around him, and even the subtle grinding of my hips, that instinctual need, rocks the boat a little bit.

The moon is out in full force, making everything sparkle in its silver hue, giving the world such an enchanting sheen.

"I've missed you," I confess urgently between kisses, my tongue warring with his. "I was so, so mad, but I couldn't turn off how much I missed you."

He's pressing down upon me as the boat wobbles back and forth, and I can feel that big, thick manhood of his pulsating with desire. For me.

With a smack of our lips, he pulls back, looks into my eyes as they glint moonlight.

"The only moment of happiness I've had these

past few months was when I saw you drive up, back into my life, Princess… Everythin' before was just passing time, tryin' to fill a void that couldn't ever be filled. I need you to be happy, babe, I need you in every which way a man can need another. And it's ingrained, right down to my marrow."

His words are deep and husky, so powerful and full of conviction.

He says them all with such passion before he lunges in and kisses me once more, his two big hands rubbing in under my shirt, feeling the swell of my belly before sliding down to work at my pants again.

There's such awe in the way he touches me, the awareness of the life we created in me so significant. But not enough to distract him from the lust we have for each other.

There's no way either of us can fight it anymore, and my hands are running over his fine, tailored suit. It feels so good, different from the usual hard denim he wears, and it makes my hand eagerly dance over it until they reach his leather belt.

I don't pause, and deep in my heart, I know we can't ever leave one another again. We can live without one another, but that's all we can do.

Just go through the motions.

His fingers are undoing my jeans as I open his suit pants. Clumsily I stand, the boat threatening to tip but he grabs hold of me, guiding me to his lap.

It's dark, but my eyes have adjusted with the dimming light, and I can see the faint outline of his cock as his pants are pulled away. As thick and large as I remember it.

He guides me on down, helping keep the boat as steady as possible.

Though once that thick crown of his is teasing along my slit and I'm moaning and squirming, we're wobbling again.

"Easy, Princess," he husks to me, holding me in his hands, guiding me on down along his shaft, letting me feel that thick girth spreading my pussy open wide again.

It's so thick! And after so long without him, it's like the first time again.

That broad shaft splaying my sex open wide, making him groan and shudder until, at last, he's embedded right to my utmost depths, pulsating wildly with his own desires.

"Ohh Abby," he husks out, his words so gravelly and hoarse. "I have missed everythin' about you… but the feel of your cunt wrapped around my cock…"

It was indescribable for us both.

I suck in a deep breath and hold it, just focusing on trying not to tip us over, but I can barely stay still.

He feels amazing, better than I even remembered it, even on those few occasions I couldn't resist anymore and touched myself to the thought of what we'd done.

My mouth is on his, and he presses back into me so hard that my lips feel sore, but I want more.

I moan into him, the sensation sending little vibrations down my tongue and into his mouth, and we try to sit still, just letting his thickness spread me open.

The rhythmic throbbing of his cock as it impales me is such a damn turn-on. It's as if that thick pole is really uniting us in body and spirit, down to even the beating of his heart.

I'm worried about how I can ride him like that, but my he takes control.

His powerful hands grip me, one on my hip and waist, the other on my ass. He lifts me up with such ease, my pussy clinging to his cock as I slide up, the two of us moaning.

Then he lets me slide back down, all of those sweet, seductively satisfying motions fully within his control.

"Ohh Princess… we were made for each other," he growls, rocking me up and down along his shaft a little faster, the smack of our bodies growing as his fingers sink into my flesh so tightly.

"There's nothin' in the world that compares to the feelin' of your lil' pussy wrapped around my cock… nothin'. Nothin' felt satisfyin' while you were away," he whispers in a husky confession, kissing at my neck, my chest. His dick throbbing wildly within me as we continued to rock from the motions.

"I couldn't even go back to before, knowing how other women pale compared to you," he growls, and maybe that's what surprises me most of all.

I clasp onto his knees, arching my back, and suddenly it's like an explosion behind my eyes. I don't know what part of me he was hitting with my body contorted like this, but I like it!

My lips hang open, and I look towards the litany of stars sparkling in the sky, and I feel like I'm soaring with them. Just the lapping of the water against the boat as Kaiden lifts and impales me, bringing me so quickly to a peak that has nearly eluded me since he left.

We're in such a public place, houses dotting the lake, but it feels like it's just us, in our own private, perfect world.

I can feel his manhood pulsating, stretching me with each new throb, though all my focus is torn away as he brings his thumb on down to rub at my clit. That hard digit circling my sensitive little bud, prodding and teasing it as he continues to move my whole body, making me ride him up and down with only minimal help from me.

"I need you Abby," he says in almost a growl. "I've needed you all the while you were gone… I need you to make me happy. I need you to get off," he says through strained words as he moans aloud, his own pleasure mounting so rapidly as I bob atop his dick.

We're in such a precarious situation, something I'd almost see as comical if not for the fact that I'm running purely on blind passion. Excitement and hope has combined within me along with the carnal passion, and I grind into his hand.

It only takes a few bliss-filled moments for me to hit that point of no return, but when I do, there's no holding back. There's no stopping the fact that I'm jerking like a mad woman, that my legs are kicking and I'm holding onto Kaiden for dear life as my orgasm strikes through my core.

Heat rises up between my thighs, wetness coating him as my fragrance becomes richer in the air, and I scream into the night.

"Yes! Kaiden!" My voice is heavy with lust and desire, my entire body exploding in pleasure, all because of him.

He's in control of it all, of me and my movements, of the boat and himself.

Yet as I lost all claim on reality to spasm and climax atop his cock, he soon after joins me.

He arches back his head and lets loose a loud wail, his own feet kicking out as I feel him swell and blow his load into me.

There's no longer any womb for him to fertilize, because he'd already more than taken care of that. But it's so satisfying nonetheless, and together we're lost to a sea of pleasure amid a placid lake of memories.

He bucks up into me wildly as he shoots each thick, creamy jet of come, and we're rocking almost as chaotically, the boat precariously close to tipping over as we both lose all our wits.

The passion that unites us, though, is not rational or logical, and we simply use one another's bodies, so desperate to find the thing that we'd once more turned our back on. Months we'd lost, but our love had only burned brighter in the absence of one another.

There's no more turning back or denying what we are to one another, what we need to be, and I milk his cock of every bit of come I can, absolutely ravenous to feel his pleasure run through me.

Kaiden lunges for me again, and he's kissing and suckling upon my neck, the two of us utterly ravenous for each other.

Though in our heedless passion, we lose sight of what we're doing, and the boat rocks too far...

Just too far enough.

And we're toppling over into the inky black night waters together, our two bodies still tangled up and enjoined.

It's only a brief moment of submersion before the two of us bob our heads up above the surface, gasping and wet. The lifejackets make it easy to stay afloat, however, and we're grinning at each other like foolish kids again.

Kaiden reaches out, wraps his arms back around me and pulls me in close, so our bodies touch once more.

"Can't say we're in over our heads at least," he remarked with dry humor in that most wet of situations.

And even though I'm sullied and soaking, and the uptight little-miss-Princess part of me might've been pissed, all I can do is laugh, my wet mouth finding his once more as we entangle our bodies in the water. It's freezing and my skin immediately goosebumps, but as his tongue presses against mine, I feel like all my cares and worries have simply... disappeared.

Kaiden holds me in his strong arms, and with the aid of the lifejackets and his kicking legs, we're floating and kissing, making out in the dark lake as we cling to one another.

It's not exactly ideal, and neither of us seems to know exactly how to screw in a lake at night. Though pawing at each other for warmth and comfort, we manage to find a way to make it work.

Kaiden and I lock bodies once more in the cool night waters, and it coaxes a moan from my lips as we bob upon the surface.

"I'm never gonna let you go out of my sight again, Abby," he pledges to me there in our foolish predicament. "I'm gonna be a husband… and a dad, and I couldn't be happier," he confesses before lunging for my lips, kissing me deep and hard as our wet lips smack.

There's no more doubts in my mind as we grind and tangle ourselves together that we've learned our lesson. That we won't keep fighting our perfection for one another.

I cling to him, and though we keep bobbing low and water splashes in our faces, my body's getting used to the cold temperature, in no small part because of the heat I feel for him.

I pull apart long enough to smile at him, to see the sparkle in his eyes, and I let out a small giggle.

"Oh my God, you are *loving* this," I tease, splashing some water against his face. His fine suit is ruined, my jeans are tied around my ankles, and this is definitely one of the silliest and strangest things I've ever done. But it is so damn *hot* at the same time. Because of him.

After all, our loins are still enmeshed, our bodies one, and I can feel every beat of his heart, every pulse of desire he has for me through that carnal link.

"I'm lovin' this, and I'm in love with you, Abby," he says with a grin, the two of us bobbing in the water, grinding and fucking in such a surreally different way.

It's hard to describe, it's not like any of our other

times having sex, the necessities of floating on the water make it slower paced than the usual wild rutting we do. But I can see the love in his eyes, feel the desire as we grind and slowly pump our hips together.

I wrap my arms around his neck, pressing my forehead against his as he grinds into me, my legs somehow wrapped around his waist.

My nose touches against his and I smile at him with such affection.

"We're gonna be parents, Kaiden," I whisper softly, my mouth lightly brushing against his. "We're gonna have to make up for a lot of lost time before we have a baby to deal with," I add with a wicked grin.

"A whole lotta time," he growled huskily.

Though truth is, as much as it's nice to just float and grind like that, we have to come in before long. The chill of the water is in us as Kaiden swims to shore and lifts my soggy ass up, dragging what he can find of our wet clothes with us.

"Here ya go, drink some of this," he says, heading to his motorcycle, pulling a thermos out of the back and pouring up some piping hot chocolate, handing it over to me with a smile.

I let out another laugh as I accept it, my eyes narrow at him.

"Oh, don't tell me you had this planned all along," I grin as I take a sip, and it's just like we used to make at home. Too sweet, with way too much cream.

His eyes sparkle with devious delight, and he lunges forward once more.

It's going to be a long, long night.

"Abigail Tuney, you've been my Princess and guiding light since I first met you. When I left you, there was only shadows and pain, doubt and fear. And that doubt, those fears, they didn't disappear when you came back into my life. They reignited my need to protect you, to make you mine. And so today, the best day of my life, we become one."

I'm trying not to cry, but he's making it impossible.

"I love you more than a man ever should."

It's not the wedding of my dreams, not by a long shot. My white dress is more... off-white, and I had to waddle down the aisle. We didn't really have anyone to invite to a wedding, so instead we're in Vegas, the city of sin.

It's fitting, in a lot of ways, and Kaiden looks damn fine in his tuxedo.

Becky, however, did manage to make the trip, along with her boyfriend, and she's at my side looking so excited. She's never met Kaiden before and, well, doesn't know he's technically my step-brother.

We decided to omit that from the wedding announcement.

I unfold my own vows, biting down on my lower lip to try to make sure I won't cry, but I know it's fruitless.

"When I first saw you, shirtless and jumping into the lake, I never could have known the impact you would have on my life. You were so tough, so cocky, and instantly I knew... I'm a girl that's going to fall for the bad boy. And I did fall, hard. Over, and over, and over again." I lick my lips, my voice quivering and I can't go on, just smiling at him, and then the marriage commissioner.

"Well, if that's all, you may now kiss the bride!" he announces, and suddenly I'm in Kaiden's arms, his hands knit through my hair, absolutely destroying my careful updo as his mouth presses against mine. It's a bruising sort of kiss, his actions so hard and passionate.

It's not the happily ever after I expected, but I couldn't imagine it being more perfect.

* * *

THANK you so much for reading! I hope you enjoyed <3 If you have a moment, please leave a review. Other readers are dying to know what you thought.

I have plenty more bad boy romance for you, so make sure you check out my other books on the next couple of pages, and sign up for my newsletter to be notified when I have a new release on the way!

~Alexis Abbott

<u>Romantic Suspense:</u>

HITMEN SERIES:

Owned by the Hitman

Sold to the Hitman

Saved by the Hitman

Captive of the Hitman

Stolen from the Hitman

Hostage of the Hitman

Taken by the Hitman

The Hitman's Masquerade (Short Story)

THE KILLER TRILOGY:

Book 1: Killer for Hire

Book 2: Killer Desire

Book 3: Killer on Fire

SEXY SEALs

Sweetheart for the SEAL

Sights on the SEAL

HOSTAGES:

Stealing Her

The Assassin's Heart

Killing For Her

Abducted

STEPBROTHERS:

Ruthless

Criminal

STANDALONES:

Betting on Love

Hunter's Baby

I Hired A Hitman

Vegas Boss

Rock Hard Bodyguard

Innocence For Sale: Jane

Redeeming Viktor

Romance:

Falling for her Boss (Novella)

Most Wanted: Lilly (Novella)

Bound as the World Burns (SFF)

Erotic Thriller:

THE DANGEROUS MEN SERIES:

The Narrow Path

Strayed from the Path

Path to Ruin

Alexis Abbott is a Wall Street Journal & USA Today bestselling author who writes about bad boys protecting their girls! Pick up her books today if you can't resist a bad boy who is a good man, and find yourself transported with super steamy sex, gritty suspense, and lots of romance.

She lives in beautiful St. John's, NL, Canada with her amazing husband.

facebook.com/abbottauthor

twitter.com/abbottauthor

instagram.com/alexisabbottauthor

bookbub.com/authors/alexis-abbott

pinterest.com/badboyromance

youtube.com/AlexisAbbott

ACKNOWLEDGMENTS

Thank you to my amazing Patrons. I'm constantly humbled and grateful for your support.

Ramona Cabrera
Melissa Hedrick
Virginia Swanson
Dawn Daughenbaugh
Don Doss
Stacie Currie

If you'd like to join them — and get my ebooks or paperbacks — you can find me here on Patreon.
https://www.patreon.com/alexisabbott